Heart Eyes

Heart Eyes

THE JOURNEY BEGINS

CHRISTINE JOHNSON

Cover design by Bill Francis Peralta
Interior design by Shieldon Alcasid

Published in the United States of America

ISBN:978-0-69297-435-3

Fiction / Christian / Fantasy
16.06.20

To my sister in Christ, Sandy Lane. She provided
me with constant support and encouragement
while I wrote this story. She hoped to
inspire me to finish the book by asking
for a finished manuscript as a birthday gift.
Happy Birthday, Sandy!

CONTENTS

INTRODUCTION

THIS STORY HAS been created with two very different ingredients. First, I took the idea of fantasy. I thought of darkness and light, evil and good. Then I added the ingredient of truth. I found this truth in the Word of God, the Bible. Next, I grasped a spoon of creativity, and I combined the ingredients and watched as the words and ideas began to form. Finally, I poured out this mixture upon the blank pages before me, allowing the thoughts and actions of the characters within the story to be revealed.

As you read, please remember that this story is part fantasy and part truth. There are study questions at the end to help you extract the truth from these pages. Have your Bible handy, you will need it. The truth is essential as you seek to see with your heart-eyes!

1

NOT A WISH

THE OUTER WALLS pulsed as the King of Lies entered his court. Each brick strained at the mortar that held it captive. Cracks shot across the floor, creating voids of blackness in the foundation. The Empire crumbled beneath the king's feet as he screamed, "The Promise!" Staggering toward his obsidian-encrusted throne, the king cried out again. This time, yelling at the hideous-faced demons within the court. "Do something!"

Ecnagorra locked eyes with the king. His stature alone demanded attention from the other demons. His evil presence was so vile that even the air departed before him as he rose to speak. He approached the king's throne and then bowing low, he intoned, "At your service, my king."

"The Promise is upon us. This is merely a foreshadowing of its fulfillment," the king quietly uttered. "It must not be fulfilled!"

"My king," Ecnagorra said, choosing his words carefully. "Can you tell me more about this Promise that you speak of?"

"The Scriptures of the Light," the king whispered.

"The forbidden lies of the enemy?" Ecnagorra whispered back, guarding his tone so as not to question the king's sanity.

The king continued. "We must find the source. I need you to find out who the enemy is sending the Promise through. According to the scriptures, if it is allowed to be fulfilled, it will destroy our kingdom."

"My king," Ecnagorra said with fire flashing from his eyes, "a small tremor or a simple earthquake should not cause such alarm, but to set your mind at ease, I have a plan. Allow me to scour the perimeter of our kingdom, looking for evidence of the enemy. Then I will report back to you on the veracity of this claim."

A low garbled growl escaped the king's thin black lips as he lashed out. "Set my mind at ease!" Lunging at Ecnagorra's black flesh, he screamed, "You fool!"

Ecnagorra fell backward to avoid the blow, but he did not move quickly enough. His scab-encrusted neck took the brunt of the lashing. His wicked form fell down onto the quaking floor.

The king let out a hideous laugh as he dipped his talon in Ecnagorra's blood. Mercilessly, he turned to the stone wall and scratched out his edict. "Go!"

Charlie flew up the stairs to his room, grabbing his backpack, jacket, and water bottle from various piles on the floor. Checking his bag, he quickly took inventory. "Map, money, and food," Charlie said out loud. "I sure hope that is enough to last me for a week." Charlie put on his jacket and backpack and reminded himself that he would need to grab the tent and the sleeping bag without his little sister seeing him. Muttering under his breath, "She is such a tattletale." Bounding down the stairs, he ran outside to falsely tell his little sister he was going to spend the night at his friend, Paul's house.

"Look, Charlie!" Sarah yelled when she saw him in the backyard. "Look, it's the last one! I'm going to catch it!" Sarah ran after the fluffy flower seed floating on the fall breeze. "I can catch it! I can!"

"Sarah!" Charlie yelled, as he ran toward his sister. "Be careful!" In her eager pursuit of the floating seed, Sarah was running straight toward the hundred-foot drop-off on the edge of their property. "Sarah!" Charlie said, as he grabbed for her before she fell into the tangle of blackberries that grew at the edge. Forcing his arm around her thin frame, he pulled her back just in time. They tumbled onto the grass.

"There it goes! I could have caught it! Why did you do that Charlie?" Sarah whined, as she got up and stomped away. "All the wishes are gone now! That was the last one!"

"They are just flowers seeds, Sarah!" Charlie huffed as he sat down on the ground while his heart pounded within his chest. "Why is it so important that you catch one anyhow?"

"I need to make a wish!" Sarah whimpered.

"Why?" Charlie asked.

"I can't tell you," Sarah answered. "Wishes have to be kept secret. You know that."

Charlie sighed. Sometimes being five years older than his little sister was just a pain. But the game had always been that Charlie would catch as many wishes as he could. When Sarah was younger, it was one of the few things that would change her tears to giggles and grins. Now she was old enough to chase them for herself and had almost gotten hurt. "Sarah, wishes aren't real."

"Yes, they are, Charlie!" Sarah said. "Wishes are special prayers that fly on the wind to the ears of God! When he catches them, he makes the prayers and wishes come true!"

"Where did you hear that?" Charlie asked.

"That's what you told me! Don't you remember?" Sarah looked sadly toward the edge of the cliff. "They really are wishes that will come true, aren't they?" She continued to stare wistfully, willing her brother to give her a better answer.

"Sarah, just tell me your wish. Maybe I can make it come true," Charlie said, finally getting up off the grass and dusting himself off.

"No. This is a special wish that only God can make come true. But I need to wish it and send it on its way to his ears." Sarah looked up at Charlie. "Can you get me another one?"

Charlie realized his little sister had just given him the excuse he needed. He now had the perfect opportunity to disappear. "Okay," Charlie said. "I will get you one. But remember that the plant that has all the extra wishes is really far down into the woods. I will probably need to spend the night in the woods, since I won't be able to get there and get back in one day." Charlie smiled at his sudden cunningness, as he continued telling the lie. "But mom would worry if she thought I was in the woods. So I will need your help. I need you to tell her that I am spending the night at Paul's house. Okay?"

"Lie for you, Charlie?" Sarah questioned, as her eyes began to tear up. "I don't want to lie…but I do need a wish."

"Sarah, it is the only way I can get you a wish. Do you want it or not?" Charlie said impatiently, as he towered over his little sister. "You said you had to have one."

"I need God to answer me," Sarah said. "When do you think you will be back?"

Charlie had never lied so much in his life, but he continued on with the fake story, rationalizing that his mom did not deserve any better. "Tell Mom I am at Paul's tonight, and I will see if I can get you your wish by tomorrow afternoon." Charlie realized that his little sister would be devastated, but he wouldn't be around to see her tears. He would be well on his way to Alaska by this time tomorrow. He was running away to go live with his uncle, Joe.

Sarah nodded her head in agreement, and Charlie quickly went to the garage to grab his tent and sleeping bag. With one last check of his backpack and supplies, he crossed the road while waving good-bye to Sarah. He stopped briefly to peer down the trail that he knew well from all the time he and his friends had spent exploring there last year. Charlie whispered his plan to himself, "I'll make it to the big old stump tonight. It will be able to provide enough shelter from any rain. Then tomorrow, I will cross over it to the other side of the ravine, find the road, and catch a ride to the train station. Soon, I will be off to Alaska and away from this mess! Go ahead and let them get a divorce! I don't have to be part of it!"

"Charlie!" a small voice pierced his thoughts. "I can't wait to get my wish!" Sarah's yellow dress waved softly in the cool evening breeze, as she stood on the other side of the gravel road.

"Sarah, I'm just getting started! Now go up to the house, it's getting dark!" Charlie waved and then abruptly took a few steps down the trail, so he could disappear from his sister's sight.

"Freedom!" He sighed. The fresh air welled around him and invited him further down the trail. Just as he was settling into a rhythm, he tripped and fell to the ground. "Ouch!" Moaning as he sat up, he rubbed his elbow and dusted himself off. As he looked around to see what he had tripped on, the glint of a metal stick caught his eye. He dug around until he could get his finger under the dirt enough to pull it up. For the moment, the great Alaskan plan was forgotten. He pulled and dug until the entire end was exposed. The end alone was the size of a doorknob. He continued to dig around until he was able to free the whole object.

"It's a key!" he exclaimed. Examining it, he could see it was an old fashioned kind of key that someone might use as a key to the city or a key to a castle on TV. Charlie began to dig the encrusted dirt out of the crevices and then carefully washed the dirt away with water from his water bottle. "It's beautiful!" Charlie said, as he admired the stunning jewels that adorned the large ornate handle. "This is probably worth something," Charlie said to himself. "Might come in handy if I need more money on my trip. I could sell it!"

He was just about to store it away in his backpack when a fading beam of the setting sun caught the jewels, and the most stunning rainbow appeared before him. "This would be worth a ton of money!" Charlie exclaimed. He turned to continue down the trail. "What?" Charlie stepped back, startled. Right in the middle of the formerly empty trail, he saw a door. Thinking he might have hit his head a little too hard in the fall, he shook himself to see if the door remained. The door did not move. Then he pinched himself, in case he was dreaming. "Ouch! Bad idea," he muttered to himself, as he massaged his arm. "A door suddenly appears and I happen to have a key. This has got to be a dream or I'm hallucinating. Whatever! Might as well try it."

He placed the key into the lock and was swept up into a violent wind. "Help!" he screamed, as he was hurtled through the air and set down just as quickly. Charlie trembled with fear as he looked around. "Okay, I think I am okay. I still have my backpack. This is just some weird dream. Don't panic."

Taking a deep breath, he continued his journey down the winding trail; at first, with a slow jog, then breaking into a full run, hoping to make it to the stump before it got too dark. Suddenly, his foot caught on something again. This time, his whole body was thrust forward, and he went facedown into the earth. He slid along the muddy ground until his head hit a log on the edge of the trail. Charlie moaned, as he struggled to get up. "I just need to sit down for a minute and rest," he said to himself. He looked around and saw a welcoming old tree a few steps away and slid down, resting his back against the gnarled trunk. Charlie took out his water bottle and began to splash water into his eyes. As the water dribbled down his face, he started to inspect his throbbing leg with bleary eyes. He could feel it beginning to swell, leaving an impression that rows of splinters were now imbedded in his socks.

Charlie screamed as his vision began to clear, and he saw what looked like a trap on his ankle. "I tripped on an old animal trap!" Charlie moaned with exasperation. "It shouldn't be this difficult to run away to Alaska!" Reaching down with his scraped hands and still trying to see through bleary eyes, he groped around for the trap to pull it off his leg. "Where is it?" He could not feel it with his hands, but he had seen it with his eyes. Stumbling to a standing position, Charlie wobbled over to a different tree and slid down again. After trying a few times to remove the trap that he could see but apparently wasn't really there, he decided it must be part of the weird dream he was having or a negative effect of hitting his head.

After a few minutes, Charlie decided to continue his journey slowly and more carefully. "Better to get there in one piece than to not get there at all!" Standing up and grabbing his backpack, Charlie's eyes caught a tiny flicker of light. "Oh, yeah, the key!" Charlie picked it up and stuffed it securely in his backpack. "Okay, slower this time!" he said to himself. "Oh, no!" he said, as he stopped after just a few steps. More black traps and snares covered the trail. He could see that someone had buried them under the leaves trying to hide them, but the persistent wind of the area had uncovered many of them. Darkness was blanketing the trail as Charlie said, "What can this be? Are my eyes playing tricks on me? Do I just need to wake up?"

Looking down, he saw the black trap still wrapped around his ankle, and now, it seemed to be holding him in one spot on the trail. "I wish I knew how to make it go away!" Charlie felt a breeze rustling through the trees, but this time, the wind seemed to be speaking.

Not a wish…but a prayer

Charlie listened closely, repeating what he thought he heard. "Not a wish…but a prayer. Not a wish…but a prayer. What? Sarah, is that you?" Charlie remembered what he had told his little sister, Sarah about the wishes. He looked at his ankle again, and instead of wishing it would go away, he prayed, "God, I know I should not have had Sarah lie to Mom about tonight. But I really need your help now. I've got some weird thing going on with a snare or a shadow that looks like a trap, and I need you to help me to get rid of it. I don't know what it is or even if it is real. I just need your help."

Still focused on his ankle and the trap, Charlie saw a hand reach for his ankle. It was made of radiant light, as it reached out and grasped the trap from Charlie's ankle. The hand crushed it in a tight fist, and when the hand opened up, the trap was gone. Fascinated by what he had just seen, Charlie watched as the hand moved up and away from the trail. A glowing river of sparkling dust followed it until it disappeared into the shadows, leaving only a fading light behind.

"I don't know what is going on," Charlie whispered, as he sat down. He tried to think about what he was seeing. He tried to figure out if he was dreaming, injured, or the shadows were just making things look weird. He had to be dreaming, he just had to be! Standing up and trying to decide what the best way to wake himself up would be, Charlie began clapping his hands and yelling at himself. "Wake up! Wake up!"

"Must you be so noisy?" a deep voice questioned.

"Who's there?" Charlie asked shakily, as he dropped his backpack with the key still in it and quickly hid behind a tree. "Who's there?" he asked again. This time, more confidently.

"You will need this," the voice whispered, as Charlie watched the key lift up from where he had stashed it and began to float toward him.

"Wha—what is going on?" Charlie stammered.

"You will need this key to unlock the truth," the voice said.

Charlie grabbed the floating key from the invisible force that handed it to him and stuffed it in his pocket. The figure became visible and towered above Charlie's small frame. Light spilled from the being, covering the young boy and lighting the formerly dim trail. "What is going on?" Charlie asked. "Who are you? Are you going to hurt me?"

"Charlie, I am here to help you become equipped for your journey," the voice said.

"My journey? How do you know about my journey? It's a secret! Not even Sarah knows I'm running away. Who are you?" Charlie's voice was laced with panic, as he struggled to understand what was happening.

"My name is Guardian. For a little while, you have been granted the ability to view the unseen spirit world, and I will be your guide on this journey. What has been concealed from your eyes will now be visible with your heart-eyes."

"But I don't want to see things!" Charlie protested. "I was just trying to get to Alaska to live with my uncle. I don't want to be a part of my parents' stupid divorce. Weekend visits, custody, the whole thing is stupid—I won't be a part of it!"

Charlie turned to start walking toward the trail that led to the stump. "It's gone! Where is the trail?" he screamed in desperation. "I need to wake up."

"Charlie, you are not dreaming," Guardian whispered. "I am here to assist you on your journey. Please let me help you."

"Oh, you don't need that old loser!" a sharp piercing voice screeched. "I'll help you do whatever you want Charlie."

Charlie covered his ears when he heard the voice, but he turned to see who it came from. "Where are you?" Charlie questioned nervously.

A figure rose out of one of the snares on the trail. It started as a dark twisting root as it rose from the ground, then it turned into a sturdy, impressive man with powerful arms. "I am Ecnagorra, a friend."

Charlie fell backward. "Get away!"

"I'd like to be your friend," Ecnagorra said. "You can trust me. How can I help you?"

"Charlie! Don't listen to him," Guardian warned. "He's not planning anything good!"

Charlie studied the two figures before him. Guardian was still emitting brightness from a seemingly inner light source that pulsed waves into the darkness. The other figure was a handsome, strong man with muscles that made his shirt fit tightly against his arms and chest. Charlie shivered in the fall breeze and was about to speak, when Ecnagorra pulled a black cape out of thin air and tossed it toward Charlie, which wrapped around his small shoulders and gave an immediate sense of heavy warmth. "You will be much more comfortable now. Now where did you say you wanted to go? The old stump? I know right where that is!"

"Yes," Charlie answered. "The old stump. How did you know about that?" Charlie immediately felt more at ease. He ran his fingers over the red stitching on the front of the cape, noticing there was a name woven into the fabric. He began to trace each letter with his fingers, the simple motion soothing him. "Ecnagorra, the trail is gone. I don't know where it went."

"Stop!" Guardian commanded. "You may not take the boy."

"He's mine now, notice the cape?" Ecnagorra said, pointing to the boy. "All mine!"

"Charlie!" Guardian yelled, "Pull off the cape now! You must get free of Ecnagorra's power!"

"He is my friend. He gave me this cape to keep me warm. I feel so warm, and I don't think I need your help anymore," Charlie answered, almost hypnotically.

Guardian sighed. "It has begun already."

"Leave us alone, old man," Ecnagorra said, as he pointed the boy down a different path. "You heard him, he does not want your help!"

Shadows pressed in making the trail extremely narrow.

"Ecnagorra, this doesn't look familiar. Are you sure this is the right way?" Charlie questioned.

"It's a shortcut, kid. Trust me," Ecnagorra hissed with a sly smile. "We will be at our destination before you know it!"

2

ECNAGORRA

"DID YOU FIND the Promise?" the King of Lies growled when a group of three figures approached his throne.

Pride stepped forward stiffly, black blades adorned his spine with a smaller row, covering the back of each leg. Ebony rods hung from his belt, each one echoed piercingly in the otherwise silent expanse. The other two creatures retreated from the king's question. Their slinking figures became no more than heavy shadows in the room.

"Answer me, Pride!" the King of Lies demanded.

Pride knelt slowly, presenting himself to the king. "There is a boy sent from the enemy. We assume the Promise will be fulfilled through him. The boy is with Ecnagorra right now, on the way to the pit. Your plans will soon be accomplished, your majesty." Turning to the two shadowy companions that lay shuddering on the floor, Pride let out a scorching breath, causing flames to dance upon their forms. "No thanks to these two!"

The King of Lies studied the countenance of Pride, wondering if the information was accurate. Pride's deeply scarred face gave no hint of any question, so the King of Lies decided to believe him for now. The king questioned, "I sent out three demons to assist Ecnagorra. Why is it only one can approach my throne?"

"These two hid behind trees when they saw that Guardian was the boy's angel." Pride stared at the two quivering shapes on the floor. "I took a snare of fear and bound the boy, long enough for Ecnagorra to catch up. Even though Guardian removed the snare, Ecnagorra was still able to capture the boy with his cape." He carefully stood up before the king. "At your eternal service, my king."

The king motioned to his salivating court assistants—who anxiously awaited any command—and charged, "Destroy the cowards!"

Six large court assistants stepped forward, each wearing a dull black armor. Surrounding the two trembling companions, each assistant roared, as their saliva turned to flames and vaporized the two shadowy forms.

The King of Lies surveyed his court and inhaled the acrid smoke, as the pleasure of the moment began to sink in. "Let that be a reminder to anyone who fails to advance evil within my kingdom! You shall not fear the messengers of the Light." Turning to Pride, the King of Lies commanded, "Now go verify that the Promise will remain unfulfilled!"

"As you have commanded, my king," Pride said, vanishing triumphantly into the air.

The weight of the cape pressed hard against Charlie's small frame, crushing his shoulders. A sharp chill shot up Charlie's spine, and he screamed, "Ecnagorra! Help me!"

Ecnagorra slowed his pace, as Charlie crumpled and fell to the ground in anguish.

Charlie's shoulders felt like something was invading his skin. A sharp sting, followed by increasing twinges of pain moved from his shoulders to his back then to his chest. His small torso throbbed as tremors wracked his body. "Make it stop! Please help me! I can't walk. My back! My back!" Charlie flailed on the ground, as the musky cape engulfed him.

"Yes, it is all just part of the process," Ecnagorra answered, as he found a log to sit on. "We'll just wait here a moment. Soon, you will become numb to the pain."

After several minutes, Charlie discovered the pain had subsided, and he could stand up. "What was that? What happened?"

"Let's just call it part of the growing process," Ecnagorra said, pointing down the trail. "Now continue!"

"Are you sure about this shortcut?" Charlie asked, as he looked around. "This does not look familiar at all, and the trail is getting too steep."

"Oh, perhaps we should make sure," Ecnagorra said with a crooked smile. Pulling a door out of the air and placing it on the trail, he asked, "Where is the key? I need it."

Charlie stood frozen to his spot. *This guy pulls doors and capes out of thin air. Is he to be trusted?*

"The key!" Ecnagorra demanded.

Charlie reached into his pocket and handed the key to Ecnagorra. "Here, just take it!"

Ecnagorra grabbed the key, but as soon as his hand touched it, a fire ignited and engulfed his entire hand. "Aaah! It's burning me, take it back! Take it back!"

Charlie was horrified, as he watched Ecnagorra's hand melting and dripping dark blood all over the key and the trail. "No!" he screamed, "I don't want to get burned too!"

"It won't burn you!" Ecnagorra shouted, as he tried to shake loose from the fire.

"Are you sure?"

"Do it now!"

Charlie carefully reached out for the key and peeling it away from Ecnagorra's palm, Charlie retrieved the key without getting burned. "Wow, you were right! It didn't burn me at all. Why not?"

Ecnagorra looked around and cursed the air, angry that he was not able to secure the key. "Apparently, you have some friends with you."

"I don't see anyone."

Ecnagorra screamed, "Trust me!" Then he began wrapping his wounded hand in cloth ripped from his own cape.

Charlie saw that wherever Ecnagorra's blood had spilled on the trail, there was a pulsating light. Then he saw Guardian placing a glimmering sword back into its sheath. "Did you do that?" Charlie asked Guardian.

Rising to his full stature, the mighty angel said, "The Truth caused that result. Ecnagorra cannot handle the truth."

"He is mine!" Ecnagorra shouted. Then turning to Charlie, he pushed the young boy down the trail, causing him to fall on his face as the key tumbled into the underbrush. "You have no power where I am taking the boy! He wears my cape, and he is mine!"

Charlie tried to get up. His face was bleeding and his eyes were blurry with dirt.

Ecnagorra pushed Charlie back down into the earth and held him there with a foot. "Stay down, while I slay your guardian!"

Guardian lunged toward Ecnagorra, quickly wrapping his enormous hand around one of the demon's feet and twisting it until it snapped.

Ecnagorra screamed and cursed, as his foot was crushed in the hands of the mighty angel.

"You know that the victory is already ours, Ecnagorra. Your kingdom will fall, and you will be cast into the abyss. Now let me have the boy and go enjoy the last moments of your freedom."

Charlie cried out, reaching for Guardian, "Please help me, I was wrong! I've made a mistake! I don't know where Ecnagorra is taking me but—"

"Silence!" Ecnagorra roared, sliding out of the mighty angel's grip and limping over to the side of the young boy. He grabbed the back of Charlie's cape and raised him to his feet. Shooting fire from his mouth, Ecnagorra declared, "The boy belongs to me, and it is you who will be defeated!"

"Help me!" Charlie cried out, as the limping Ecnagorra dragged him deeper down the trail. Charlie winced in pain as black snakes slithered out of the underbrush along the trail and grabbed at his ankles. Struggling to gain his footing, Charlie yelled, "Help me! Please help me!" Charlie felt something brush against him and looking down, he saw the key being tucked safely in his pocket. "Thank you," Charlie whispered to the invisible Guardian. "I will keep the key close to me."

"I'll take care of your guardian later," Ecnagorra hissed, shoving Charlie down the trail. "He will be of no help to you where you are going."

Charlie looked around, as he stumbled down the steep trail. *Not a wish…but a prayer. Lord, I need your help. Please help me.*

"Silence!" Ecnagorra screamed at the boy, "That hurts my ears!"

"I didn't say anything," Charlie said.

"Never mind, just keep going," Ecnagorra gave the boy another push down the trail.

Charlie grabbed at the cape, pulling wildly to be free of it. To his horror, he felt the roots burning their way into his body. Every effort he made to be released was met with intense pain.

Ecnagorra allowed a hideous laugh to escape his thin lips. "Go ahead and scream and flail to try to free yourself from my power! You will never succeed. Don't you get it? The cape claims you as my property. Don't you see the name on the front? That is my name, and now you belong to me! It is just a matter of time before the roots take a firm hold upon your heart. But don't worry, I will lead you to a place where you can scream all you want!" Ecnagorra threw back his head, his red eyes flashing. "No one will hear you! No guardian can save you there."

While still pulling, Charlie looked down at the lettering on the cape. What was the name printed on it? He tried to make out each letter. A was the first letter written large and ornate across the top of the cape. Charlie grabbed the edge of the cape and tried to bring the name closer to his face so he could read it. Blood dripped from his raw fingers, as he clutched a fist full of fabric in his hands and ripped a small a hole in the fabric. *So it can rip,* he thought, pulling at the bottom hem. *Oh, Lord, please help me remove this cape, even if it is only piece by piece!*

"Stop!" Ecnagorra screamed, pushing Charlie violently into a large rock on the trail. Charlie lay motionless and unconscious. "Finally, some silence!" Ecnagorra said reaching down and grabbing the neck of the cape. Ecnagorra dragged Charlie the rest of the way down the trail. As he reached the pit, Ecnagorra hoisted Charlie up and threw him into the deep hole, listening as the boy splashed into the sludge that filled the Pit of Despair. Slamming the doors of bondage closed, Ecnagorra bound the entrance with chains of Anger and Frustration.

A violent wind caught Ecnagorra's cape, as he declared, "You have been stopped! No one can come to your rescue here!" There will be no Promise fulfilled!"

3

THE WORK OF PRAYER

C HARLIE WOKE UP immediately. He was sinking into a thick liquid that surrounded him. As Charlie thrashed to stay afloat, he began reaching out for anything to grab on to. It was so dark, he could not even see his own hand in front of his face.

"Help!" Charlie cried. "God help me!" Charlie continued to move, but soon, his arms and legs were refusing to do the work to stay afloat. "Oh God, are you just going to let me die? Where are you? I just need something to stand on. All I need is—" Charlie screamed as his foot struck a rock beneath him. Kicking his left foot toward the rock again, he managed to get both of his feet positioned upon the rock and sighed. "Thank you, God…what?" Charlie lurched back and hit the wall of the pit behind him, losing his footing entirely. Struggling to find the rock again, he was finally able to regain his footing. Something had caused a small explosion of light in the pit. Looking up, he said, "God, what made the light? Please help me to know what made the light. There was light! Did I imagine it?"

Charlie reached up and rubbed his throbbing head. Was he hallucinating? His bloody hand moved from his forehead on to his shoulders, and for the first time, he realized the cape was still causing intense pressure upon him. Charlie felt the roots growing deeper toward his heart. "I should have listened to Guardian. What was I thinking? God, I am sorry. I don't know why I'm doing the things I'm doing. Can you please help me? I—I am really sorry! Thanks for sending Guardian and…what?" The air lit up again. "How do I get some more light, God?" Charlie tried to remember what he had been saying when he saw the air light up and started repeating the words one by one to see if perhaps one of the words had made the difference. "God…help…sorry…thanks…" The air lit up again with fragments of light, which allowed Charlie to see for a brief moment. "Thanks!" Again, the air lit up. "Thanks! Thanks, thanks, thanks, and thanks again!" Charlie watched each word as it moved out into the darkness and then exploded into crystals of light, allowing him to see. Charlie could see! "Okay, Lord, now please show me how to get this cape off."

"Call it by name," a voice said.

"What? Who said that? Who is there?" Then Charlie heard it again.

"Call it by name." A voice so quiet yet so strong, it was almost a whisper—more like a breeze floating through his head.

Charlie glanced down at the cape and remembered there *was* a name on it in beautiful red lettering. Pulling the cape toward his eyes, Charlie began to sing a praise song so that there would be enough light in the pit to read the name embroidered on the cape. Finally, Charlie put all the letters together A-R-R-O-G-A-N-C-E! "Thank you, Lord, for showing this to me! I say, arrogance be gone!" Charlie could feel the roots begin to retreat. His whole body cringed. "Be gone, Arrogance!" he cried again. "Be gone!" The cape eventually lost its ability to control the boy and slid off, sinking into the deep pit. Charlie wept, as he felt freedom from the pressure and pain that had been placed upon his shoulders. "Thank you! Thank you! Thank you!"

The King of Lies anxiously awaited news about the boy. The quaking in his kingdom had almost stopped; only small underlying tremors still shook the foundation of the court. Looking up, the king saw Ecnagorra limping into his court. "Enter and tell me of your journey with the boy. Is he in the Pit of Despair?"

"Yes, my king." Ecnagorra bowed unsteadily, as he balanced on his good foot. "The Promise, as you call it, cannot be fulfilled."

"As *I* call it?" the king screamed, shooting a fiery stream toward Ecnagorra. "You are dismissed! Be gone!"

Ecnagorra did not move but dared to ask, "Doesn't it seem strange a mere child can cause such disruption?"

"Fool!" The king spat at Ecnagorra. "Do you not yet realize children are the most powerful weapon our enemy has?" Still seething, the king continued. "A child filled with faith can resist our curses. But a child of faith and wisdom, *that* is the most feared kind. This child had to be stopped before he realized the power of the Promise."

"My king," Ecnagorra said. "Do not worry. Our work and your power will remain unhindered. He is defeated under the curse of my cape and my power."

"What about the Guardian?" the king questioned.

Ecnagorra lied, "He has been slain and bleeds upon the trail to the pit. I left his body as a sign to the other angels that may be in the area. Now they will know that they have no chance here in our kingdom. Our evil will always defeat their swords!"

"I expected no less," the king answered. "Have the roots of arrogance reached the boy's heart yet?"

"Soon, my king, soon." Ecnagorra smiled, bowing again as he began to exit, feeling superior to the king.

A small shriek pierced the air, and a scout demon ran in, leaving the heavy doors that guarded the king's courts open. The trembling demon approached immediately prostrating himself out in front of the king's throne. "Make it stop, your majesty! Make it stop! The whole kingdom is in pain. Everyone is screaming and holding their heads! My king, I beseech thee, make it stop!"

The king looked perplexed. Glancing up, he noticed each member of his court grabbing his or her head and moaning in pain. He then instinctively clutched his own head, as a searing pain shot deep within him. The king yelled, "This is the work of prayer! Ecnagorra, prayer from the boy is being felt far and wide in my kingdom. I thought you had him under your power? I thought the roots were taking hold of his heart? Silence the boy, once and for all!" The king stood up, as flames from the court assistants began shooting and engulfing Ecnagorra. "Go! Stop the boy!" The king commanded.

"I will go and silence the boy once and for all," Ecnagorra replied from his now disfigured face and blistered body. He left the court limping, leaving a bloody trail and gripping his own head in pain.

Even the scout demons joined in and glared at Ecnagorra, once a mighty demon, now a mutilated wretch. "Failure!" the group began to chant, as they hurled red-hot stones at him. "Be gone, before we vaporize you!"

Ecnagorra stumbled out of the court and down the trail that led to the Pit of Despair. When he was close, he could see the heavy doors that covered the top of the pit were moving up, as if being pressed from within. He froze and watched in horror. *How did the boy know? Had the Guardian been here?* The heavy chains of bondage that had secured the pit were now stretching to their full limit and began to separate. Each link of Anger and Frustration was separating and losing its power to bind the opening to the pit.

"Hey, Ecnagorra," a voice behind him said. "Is that the boy who is believed to bring the Promise?"

"Yes," Ecnagorra answered, as he watched the doors being pressed even further toward their breaking point. "Who are you?"

"I am a scout, sent by the king to verify that the boy stops praying." The small scout demon approached Ecnagorra and stood next to his bloodied, blistered frame. "I know that prayer hurts our ears, but what is the golden power that pushes at the gates of the pit?"

Ecnagorra knew that his life would be over if the King of Lies discovered the true situation. He would have him cast into the abyss. Defeated, Ecnagorra explained, "That is praise. It is the secret weapon of the enemy. The power of the Maker of Light resides in praise. The Maker has lit up the darkness of the pit for the boy. Now as the boy continues to praise the Maker, the praise power is breaking the chains of Anger and Frustration that I secured him with. I am sure that the cape of Arrogance has been identified and rebuked by now. The boy will emerge from the Pit of Despair. It is simply a matter of time."

"But if he escapes, what will happen? Will he continue to pray? Will he continue to praise? What will become of our kingdom if the boy is free to move about?" The small scout demon trembled as he questioned Ecnagorra. "Is our king in danger?"

Ecnagorra paused, weighing his words carefully. Pointing toward the chains that were seconds away from breaking, Ecnagorra said, "I don't know what will happen. I just know that the king will not allow me to live to see it."

Inside the pit, Charlie continued to sing songs of praise, laughing, and thanking God, as he watched the power of God push open the heavy doors. Charlie was learning how powerful God really was. More powerful than the enemy, who had tried to hurt him, and more powerful than despair, anger, or frustration. *God can do anything!* Suddenly, the bondage that had held Charlie in the pit broke free, and he climbed out.

Exhausted, he stood up, wiping off the rest of the black goo of Despair. Looking around, he noticed a small pile of ashes and one figure moving away in the distance. Charlie checked to make sure the key was still in his pocket and scrambled toward the trail, praying as he ran.

"I don't know what is ahead of me, Lord, but I do know that I can trust you to help me. Please help me to get back home. I won't run away again. Thank you for setting me free!"

As Charlie ran up the hill, he felt the Lord speaking to him, "Take the path of light." Overwhelmed with gratitude, he stopped in a small clearing and dropped to his knees in prayer. "Thank you! Thank you! Thank you!" Charlie said, as he watched the power of praise light the night. Then he sensed the Lord telling him to take the path of light again. "I'm coming home, Mom and Sarah. I'm coming home!"

Realizing he was close to the top, he suddenly saw a glowing path in front of him. *The path of light! There it is!* Charlie stopped.

A large shadowy shape moved out and stood in the trail about twenty feet ahead of him. He couldn't see it clearly because of the night, yet he felt courage and called out, "Who's there? Do not stand in my way. I have the Lord God on my side!"

The shape moved slightly, so that Charlie could see the path of light glowing behind the figure. Then it came closer to Charlie. It was now standing directly in the middle of the trail. Charlie hid behind a tree, but the shape seemed to know exactly where he was hiding and continued moving toward him.

"You may not travel this way," the black creature bellowed.

4

OL' TIE

CHARLIE'S KNEES LOCKED into place, frozen to his spot; he was even holding his breath, hoping the creature would somehow pass him by. He finally managed to speak. "But I must travel this way! I see the path of light right behind you."

"You may not pass by me!" the creature thundered, shaking the ground and echoing in every direction.

Charlie shivered and tried to make himself even smaller. "*Psst!* Over here." Charlie looked around and saw a kindly looking older man about ten feet behind him. "*Psst!* Come over here. Do you need some help?" the old man whispered again.

"Who are you?" Charlie whispered, as he moved away from the ominous black shape and toward the old man.

"My name is Tieced. But my friends call me Ol' Tie. I am a farmer." The old man chuckled, looking down at his worn overalls. "Well, I suppose you could tell that by the way I am dressed!"

"I could use some help," Charlie finally said. "I am trying to follow the path of light. I was doing fine until this big black thing stood in the middle of the trail. He said I can't go that way."

"Yes, he always guards *that* way."

"How do I get around him if he is always there?"

Ol' Tie rubbed his chin and said, "Well, if it was me, I would take the *other* way."

Charlie thought for a moment and then decided that he had better check this Ol' Tie guy out a little more, before he started taking directions from him. He looked harmless enough, wearing a shabby, red plaid shirt with rolled up sleeves and faded dirt-stained denim overalls. A pair of gloves hung out of his back pocket and a tattered red bandana was shoved in a front pocket next to one of those big square pencils that only old people use. Even his boots were covered with mud, as if he had just come from the field. "Do you mind me asking what you are doing here?"

"Good question! Smart young man you are. I have a farm close to here, and I always try to keep a look out for weary travelers. You do look weary! Maybe you would enjoy some supper at the farm, and we can take a look at those cuts and scrapes. Were you in a fight or something?" Ol' Tie asked.

"It's a long story." Charlie sighed. "How far away is your farm? I am hungry, and if I could clean up a little before I get back home, I won't worry my mom so much."

"Well, come on over then, young man!" Ol' Tie said, as he motioned down the trail. "The farm is just a short stroll from here."

"But that is where I just came from, and I did not see a farm," Charlie complained. "I don't want to go back!"

"Well, suit yourself," Ol' Tie said. "I just thought I could help you out. There was an angel that asked me to—"

"Guardian? Is he here?" Charlie looked around to see if he could find the angel.

"Well, of course he is not here!" Ol' Tie chuckled. "That's why he asked me to help you out."

Charlie looked up at the trail of light and then down the trail where he had just come from. Going backward did not seem right but his stomach was growling, and it would be great to get a little cleaned up so when he *did* get home, he would not worry his mom. The story itself would be hard enough to believe, but it might be better if he did not look so beat up. "I guess it would not hurt to go back just a little. You said there is another way. Is it far?"

"Not far at all," Ol' Tie assured him. "The farm is tucked away, down a side trail. That is why you could not see it. We'll be there 'fore you know it."

Ol' Tie was right. The farm was not far down the trail. Charlie felt he was barely going backward at all. The farm spread out before his eyes; it was so peaceful, with small green hills rising and falling in the distance. A fence surrounded one field that looked like it was covered with an unusual looking crop. Charlie remembered visiting his own grandfather's farm at harvest time and the look of the fields when they were ripe for harvest. This field did not look like anything his grandfather had grown. "What are you growing in that field over there?" Charlie asked. "Kind of looks like weeds."

"Oh, plenty of time to ask questions after we get you something to eat, my boy," Ol' Tie said, pointing to the farmhouse in the distance. "I've got a hankering for something like cookies and milk. How 'bout you?"

Charlie looked toward the farmhouse. It looked so inviting—just a small white home next to a big red barn. The whole farm seemed like a picture out of a book. "I guess I didn't realize just how hungry and tired I am. Cookies and milk sure sound good right now."

Ol' Tie moved behind Charlie and put his hand upon his back. "Yes, yes, just come with me. I'll take care of you."

Charlie felt a weight on his shoulder, right where Ol' Tie had placed his hand. "Did you put something on my back? It feels heavy where you touched me," Charlie said as he turned around and around, trying to see what could possibly be on his back. Then looking up, he noticed Ol' Tie's face had become distorted. It was as if he was wearing a mask, and it was sliding off his face. Charlie looked back up toward the farmhouse and blinked. The house seemed darker now, or was it just the sun moving behind a cloud? The house was white a minute ago, and now it appeared gray; the red barn was now hidden by murky smoke that had suddenly moved in.

"Tie, I don't feel very well. I need to stop. I can't breathe…I can't…" Charlie collapsed, as he whispered a prayer, "Lord, help me! Please help me!"

Cringing and holding his ears, Ol' Tie said, "Oh, you poor child!" Then he pulled out his red bandana and waved it in the air toward the farmhouse. "Got him!"

"Finally!" one of the demons said, slamming his clawed fist into the table

"Silence, Malice!" Folly said, spitting fire at him. "He might hear you!"

Malice growled, "I just want to know what took Deceit so long. I could have had the boy in here and disposed of by now."

Folly answered with a hideous laugh. "Don't you mean *Ol' Tie*? I can't wait to see the look of fear on the face of that child!"

When Charlie awoke, he was in a dimly lit room. Glowing red eyes stared at him from the shadows. Charlie counted the eyes, *two, four, six…yes, just six*. "Lord, please help me."

As soon as Charlie said that, he could hear moans in the shadows. "Lord, please help me!" Charlie yelled this time. Again, the moans. *I know what will make those voices scream in pain!* "Thank you, Lord for watching over me. I know that you are here with me! Thank you in advance for setting me free from this place. Thank you! Thank you! Thank you!"

As Charlie spoke, the weight he had felt upon his back dissipated and a hedge of golden powder surrounded him, completely separating him from the pairs of glowing red eyes. Charlie looked around and tried to find a door, but everything outside the buffer of praise was dark. He continued to praise and pray, and then he saw it. There was a door! Charlie quickly walked over and placed his hand on the knob, as he opened the door light flooded the room as if to usher him out.

"Oh, my boy, are you okay? You took quite a fall. I was so worried about you. Come over here, so I can take a look at your head. I fear you may have a big bump growing on that noggin of yours." Ol' Tie was standing opposite the door near another room, where an enticing smell was coming from. "I've just baked the cookies I promised you. Now come on over here, and we'll get you cleaned up so you won't be worrying your folks when you get home."

"What happened?" Charlie asked. "The last thing I remember was your face looking weird and something heavy on my back. And what is with the fiery eyes?"

Ol' Tie chuckled. "Yes, the farmhouse and I are old and not always the best-looking. Me, I'm just weathered. The house has floorboards that squeak and moan and dark corners with mysterious shadows. It's just a sad old pile of boards, but it's my home."

Charlie still had his hand on the doorknob, but that smell—it made his mouth water a little. Charlie wanted both things; he wanted to continue on his way, but he also wanted whatever smelled so delicious. God had answered his prayers. Here was a door, a way of escape. But the desire to fill the craving in his stomach was so intense. Charlie took a deep breath and allowed the delightful smell to completely fill his nose. "Ol' Tie, I have an idea. Can you pack me some of those cookies to go? I really need to get to the trail of light, and I could eat them while I am traveling." *There! Both problems solved,* Charlie thought with just a hint of pride.

"Bright boy!" Ol' Tie said as he ushered Charlie to the table where the cookies lay fresh out of the oven. "You're right. Come on over here, and we'll get you some of those delicious nuggets to bring with you on the trail!"

Charlie headed toward the other room, following the smell of freshly baked chocolate chip cookies. The door that had been opened closed with a solid thud. Charlie looked back and noticed how incredibly dark everything was once again. Ol' Tie packed up a small brown bag for Charlie and even threw in a napkin ('cause fresh chocolate can be a bit messy).

"How about you and me go check out that field you were wondering about? It is on the way to the trail."

"Thanks, but I really need to get going," Charlie said, as he grabbed the brown bag of cookies and headed toward the door. Placing his hand on the handle Charlie tried turning the knob, but what was easy just a moment ago wouldn't budge now. "Is there some sort of trick to this door?" Charlie asked pulling hard on the handle.

"Oh, that ol' thing just gets stuck now and again. The doorjamb must have swelled or somethin'."

"How do I get it unstuck?" Charlie asked, a small bit of panic rose in his throat.

"Well," Ol' Tie mused, "I suppose when it's good and ready to unswell, it will also be unstuck! That will probably be next summer!"

Charlie felt his breathing increase and his heartbeat become more rapid. Sweat began to form on the back of his neck as he nervously asked, "But how do I get out now?"

"No worries," Ol' Tie said. "Lucky for you, I've got a back door to this old pile of boards! Come on and follow me."

"Now where did that child go?" Guardian asked himself, as he walked toward the trail of light. Then he saw it, and he knew there was more trouble. The Key of Truth had been dropped again.

Ol' Tie handed a bag of warm chocolate chip cookies to Charlie, then they walked through the old farmhouse kitchen to the back door. The rickety porch creaked as they went down the steps.

Charlie could see the field—the one that looked like it was growing weeds. He reached into the bag and snatched a warm cookie. Shoving it in his mouth, he said, "So you were going to tell me about that field over there."

"Oh, yes, in due time. But first, let's get a little closer why don't we," Ol' Tie said.

The chocolate swirled around in Charlie's mouth and glided so smoothly down his throat. "*Mmm…delicious!*" he said.

"Yes, I do make a mean batch of cookies, don't I?" Ol' Tie said, as he stopped and put his arm around the boy's shoulders. "This is the field you were asking about. What do you think?"

Charlie felt that weight on his shoulders where Ol' Tie's arm was again and asked, "Why is your arm so heavy?"

"Medical condition. Now what do you think of my field? Isn't it beautiful?" Ol' Tie asked.

"Well, actually, it looks like a bunch of weeds to me. What are you growing?" Charlie asked.

"Something very tasty. Indeed, I think you will agree with me," Ol' Tie said with a sly smile.

"What do you mean?" Charlie questioned.

"The cookies! Aren't they delicious? They are filled with seeds from this field! That is what makes them so delectable!" Ol' Tie proclaimed.

"Seeds? I didn't have any seeds in my cookies," Charlie protested.

"Oh, these seeds are very small to start with. Give them time, they will grow on you," Ol' Tie assured the boy.

"What do you mean grow on me? What kind of seeds did you give me?" Charlie said, fear and panic rising again in his throat.

"The best kind! Seeds of deception!" Ol' Tie said with a hideous laugh, as he ripped off his mask and exposed his grotesque features to Charlie.

"What have you done to me?" Charlie tried to scream, but his throat was already swelling, making it hard to even breathe. *God help me! Help me, please!* Charlie prayed as everything before him faded to black.

Guardian opened the door to the farmhouse and saw Malice and Folly celebrating as they danced around the boy's body, which lay motionless on the floor. "Away from the boy!" Guardian commanded. "Be gone!"

Deception breathed a blast of fire at Guardian, who quickly turned and shot the fire back at Deception, disfiguring his face even more. "The boy belongs here with us. He is polluted now with deception! He is not fit for the Maker's plan. He belongs to us!"

"No!" Guardian shouted, as he pulled his sword from its sheath.

With a single movement, Guardian cut Malice in two and heard him shriek as he disappeared into the abyss. Folly approached Guardian from behind, throwing a black rope of fear around the mighty angel. Again, Guardian used his sword to cut through the rope and then sliced Folly right down the middle. The demon vaporized, and an acrid smoke filled the room. Then Guardian turned his full attention to Deception.

"Stop!" Deception screamed. "You may have the boy. I have accomplished my assignment. Now the harvest!" Deception screamed as he shot out of the room, leaving behind a trail of fire and sending embers raining down upon Guardian and Charlie.

5

THE SWORD

GUARDIAN LOOKED DOWN and noticed Charlie was beginning to wake up.

"Guardian? Guardian, I need help!" Charlie let out a great sigh of relief at seeing the angel. With his tongue, he found the seeds in his mouth and tried to spit them out. But they were stuck on the inside of his cheeks. Charlie reached into his mouth and tried to pull them out with his fingers, but they would not budge. The seeds had grown roots in his mouth, and now his mouth began to feel very warm—almost hot to the touch. "What have I done?" Charlie said, as he slumped back down against the floor.

"Why did you allow Deception to plant seeds within you?" Guardian glared at the small boy. "Why did you stop praying?" Guardian demanded. "I heard your prayer for help. I would have used my sword and slay the demon that blocked the trail of light. But then you grew silent and chose to handle the situation with your own plans, instead of depending upon the power of God, the power of prayer."

"I was scared! I thought I could…Oh, Guardian! What am I going to do now?" Charlie looked around him and saw that the only light now came from Guardian's presence. "What do I do? The things in my mouth are getting bigger. I need to get them out."

"The seeds within your mouth are called deception. If you do not remove them, they will continue to grow. The roots of deception will reach for your heart and plant themselves within it. Then the desires of your heart will change. You will not recognize the truth, like you do now. You will choose the darkness, instead of light. Is this what you want, Charlie? Do you want to be deceived? Do you want a life full of deception?"

"No! How do I remove them? What do I do, Guardian?" Charlie begged.

"What do you see, Charlie?"

"Right now? Nothing. Everything is black, except for you." Charlie said as he looked around, feeling the night air grow colder, yet his face was swelling with heat.

"What would make it light?" the angel questioned.

"Praise? Is that what you are getting at?"

"That is part of it. Which force is stronger? Truth or Evil?"

"Truth, I guess," Charlie said.

"You guess?" Guardian's eyes were saddened.

"No!" Charlie said, standing up. "But I don't know what to do."

"Command it to leave," Guardian said in an even tone. "Call it by name. Command it to leave in the name of Jesus!"

"But I can't!" Charlie answered. "It has roots! It will rip off part of my face!"

"I'll ask you again," the angel said. "Which is stronger? Is the truth stronger than the deception? Or is the deception stronger than the truth?"

"The truth is stronger," Charlie stated, as he put his hand up to his cheek and closed his eyes. "I am sorry, Lord. I was scared. I did not mean to allow Deception to be planted within me. Please release me from the roots of Deception, and please don't let them grow any closer to my heart. I ask these things in the name of Jesus, amen." Charlie opened his eyes and saw Guardian, also praying. "What are you asking God for?"

"I was thanking our Lord for his power over the darkness and deception," Guardian said, reaching up and pulling a sword out from under his wing. The sword glowed against the night and left a trail of light as it moved through the air. "This is the first part of your armor, Charlie. Go ahead and take it."

Charlie reached out for the sword, grasping the handle firmly in his small hands. "It is very heavy," Charlie said. "What am I supposed to do with it?"

"Remove the deception," the angel said.

Charlie could not believe the angel's words. Was Guardian really expecting him to operate on himself with this sword? Did this angel think that he would cut his face off to remove the deception? "You want me to cut the seeds out of my mouth with this sword?"

"What is it that holds the deception within your mouth?" the angel asked.

"The roots," Charlie responded. "It will not move because it has roots."

"Many things have roots," the angel answered. "Roots hold things in place. Remove the roots, and the thing—whatever it is—will lose its stronghold."

"Guardian, are you telling me to use this sword and cut the roots out of my mouth?" Charlie said as he pointed the brightly lit sword toward his mouth. "I just don't think I can do that!"

The angel knelt down to get right at Charlie's eye level. "I will say it again. Remove the deception."

"Guardian, you are a strong angel. Why can't you just take me home?" Charlie lowered his head. "I am sure you could do it if you wanted to."

"What I want to do is the will of the One who sent me," Guardian said as he stood up. "What do you want to do?"

"I want to run away from home," Charlie said as he laid the sword down on the ground. "I want to get as far away from my mom and dad as I can. I want to go to Alaska."

"Then go," the angel said, as he turned around. Guardian began to walk away then turned and said, "You have free will to follow your own thoughts and ideas. As for me, I want to please the One who sent me. The Lord asked me to help you, and that is what I am here to do. However, if you do not intend to follow the path and plans God has for you, then that is your choice." Guardian saw the sword that Charlie had thrown down upon the ground. With his eyes, he motioned in that direction. "I would suggest that you keep the Sword of Truth with you. However, it is your decision."

"What about the deception growing in my mouth?" Charlie said with desperation in his voice. "What do I do about that?"

"Didn't we pray and ask God for help?" Guardian looked sad. "Do you remember what the Lord provided for you after you prayed? It was the Sword of Truth. Like I said, you might want to hang on to that. It is a very important piece of equipment."

"Okay," Charlie said as he picked up the sword and held it in both hands, because it was so heavy. Then Charlie noticed something. When he held the sword up, not only did it light the darkness, it cooled the heat of deception. Charlie held the sword right next to his face and was surprised at the relief he felt from the pain and swelling in his face. Finally, Charlie took the sword and laid it right next to his cheek. "Please God, make this thing, this Deception, go away." Immediately, Charlie felt like the swelling was going away, almost gone. Reaching into his mouth, he decided to try to pull the seeds out. He grabbed on to one of the seeds and gave it a big tug. He felt one of the roots break off within his cheek. Now he could wiggle the seeds a little. Charlie held up the sword of truth to his cheek again and began to pray.

"Lord, I think I get it now. I ask for the truth of your power and presence to remove the roots and seeds of the Deception. I am sorry that I ate the seeds. Please forgive me for wanting to fill my desires, instead of taking the way of escape you provided for me." Charlie reached into his mouth again and pulled as hard as he could on the seeds. Gradually, he worked them out of his mouth, even the root that had broken off. Amazed at how long the roots had become, he threw them on the ground, spitting out every last piece of Deception.

Horrified, Charlie noticed that the roots and seeds that were in his mouth were now growing into the floor before him and intertwining with the wooden boards. Charlie grabbed the sword with both hands and began to cut away at the roots, chopping them into small pieces. As the sword cut into the roots, they immediately started drying up and turning to dust. Charlie finished chopping up all the roots then crushed the seeds with the tip of the sword. Finally, after everything he had touched with the sword had turned to dust, he cleared the floor of the debris and noticed Guardian was standing watching him.

"Guardian, why?" Charlie questioned. "Why when I take the easy way to freedom, it is not the right way, but the more difficult way? The path of light had obstacles."

"Tell me about the obstacle you faced. What was its name? How did it respond when you called it by name and told it to be gone?"

Charlie stammered, "I…I never really faced the obstacle. I was scared! I thought the black creature would hurt me. So I turned around and took what seemed like the easier way. Ol' Tie said he was sent by you to help me."

"This is a great lie of the enemy. First, he will instill fear to keep us from moving forward, then he will make freedom look like bondage and bondage look like freedom. The way to avoid this deception is to know the truth."

"What is this truth, Guardian?" Charlie asked. "I want to be free!"

"Charlie, come with me. We must continue on the journey," Guardian said as he knelt next to the boy. "We are on a journey, and there is something I must show you."

"You aren't helping me get to Alaska, are you?" Charlie asked.

"Is that really what you want to do? I will leave you to your own desires. But remember, the Lord is with you always!" Guardian said, as he disappeared into the blackness.

"I will bring the sword with me. But I am going to Alaska!" Charlie called out after him and then turned to continue his journey alone. After he left the farmhouse, he finally got back to the place where the enormous black shadow had been, and he saw it was gone. But so was the path of light. "Now what? Guardian!" Charlie cried out.

Collapsing against the bottom of a tree, he poured out his heart to God. "Thank you, Lord, for helping me. Thank you that Truth is so powerful."

Charlie began to think about some of the things that Guardian had said. Then he felt ashamed. All he had been thinking about was what he wanted. When he should have been asking was what God wanted. Charlie picked up the sword, stood up, and turned around. It was black, except for the light radiating from the Sword of Truth. Charlie hoped that he would not find any more black creatures, farmers, or snakes of fear. Then laughing to himself, he remembered the power of the sword he held in his hands.

"Guardian!" Charlie called out. "I'm ready to follow God's plan for my life and His path of light. I am ready to listen. Please God, please bring Guardian back to help me on the journey. I am ready to listen!" Charlie raised the sword up against the blackness and strained to see further, trying to find the path of light. Then he heard a sharp snap, like a stick breaking in the woods. Charlie called out, "Is that you, Guardian?"

6

FIND THE BOY

A SLIMY FOG MOVED through the court of the King of Lies, as he commanded a report from the spies. "Enter the king's court, and tell me what you have discovered."

The small demon raised his head, just enough so he could see where he was walking, then fell down trembling before the king. "I have news, your majesty."

"Then tell me!" demanded the king. "Do not waste my time!"

The demon shuddered, carefully choosing his words. "The boy is alone, my king. Guardian has left him."

"That seems odd," the king said, tipping his head to get a better look at the face of the trembling demon. "Why would Guardian, who was supposed to be dead, leave the young man alone? Are you lying to me?"

"No, my king. The boy is alone, but he has something with him." The small demon took a deep breath then finished his sentence. "He has the Sword of Truth with him."

The King of Lies sat silently for a moment then rising from his chair, he turned to his senior chief assistant, Shirez and said "Follow me!"

Shirez obediently followed the king into his chambers. Shirez' enormous black shadow enveloped the entire room. Made up more of a vapor than a body, the demon instilled fear easily through his massive size. "My king," Shirez said, bowing before the king. "What do you need?"

"The Promise is being fulfilled!" the King declared.

Shirez lifted his head and asked, "What Promise? The One has already come to earth and been crucified. Has he returned? Is that the Promise you speak of?"

"No. When he returns, there will be no time for discussion. However, in the end days, there is to be an outpouring of the Light's Promise. Power from the Maker of the Light himself! Many will rise who will be able to recognize it and fight us without fear. They will have learned the secrets of the vault."

Shirez stood silently for a moment and then carefully questioned the king, "I thought that the vault was a mere lie spread by followers of the Light. Is there really a vault? What secrets does it hold?"

The king grabbed Shirez by the neck and began to choke him, "I need the boy stopped before he is allowed to teach others how to fight us! Go and find him!" The king loosened his grip and allowed the weakened body of Shirez to drop to the floor. "I expect a report today. Ecnagorra has already failed at this task and received the consequences of his failure."

Shirez lifted his head and answered as best he could in a garbled voice, "Yes, my king."

The king whispered, as he looked around for any prying ears or eyes, "Have you ever read the scriptures of the Light? The Light works through those who are like children. The Light even states that a child can be the greatest in the kingdom of heaven. This child is carrying the Sword of Truth! Do you understand the power that the sword carries? Do you know what the scriptures say of it? Nothing can stop it!"

"My king, you've been reading the lies of the Light?" Shirez took a step back. "Those scriptures are banned, if anyone knew—"

"Silence!" the king commanded. "Go and find the child. He has already defeated us twice now. If progress toward the vault cannot be stopped, we will all be doomed." The king sat back. "But do not kill him yet. Yes, I want him alive."

"Why, my king?"

"Do you not yet understand the best way to overcome an adversary?" the king questioned. "You become their friend, their confidant! We will capture the boy and then train him in evil for our purposes. He will learn under my tutelage! Yes, imagine if he was on our side, teaching the youth of this world how to bind and destroy the followers of the Light!"

Shirez stepped back from the king slowly, without turning his back for fear of a flaming lashing. "Surely, my King, this child is simply a small problem to be dealt with. Do not concern yourself like this. I will find the child and bring back the reports you require. A simple gathering of demons should be able to handle a mere child. I do not see the problem."

"Just go! You will report only to me when you return. I shall be in the inner sanctum. I will not speak again to the court or to the kingdom until you return with news." The king left the chamber, slamming the door behind him.

Pondering the conversation, Shirez began making his own plans. The lies of the Light were spreading into the king's mind, and fear of the Light was taking control. *My time has come.*

Walking out into the king's court, he commanded, "I need four scouts to accomplish a small task for me."

"I will go!" one small scout demon yelled.

"And me!" another one echoed. Two more demons stepped forward and joined the group.

"Excellent," Shirez said. "You are to find the boy and then bind the boy. Use whatever methods you please. Then bring him to the king's court. This should be an easy enough task now that Guardian has left him. When you return, you will report to me. Only to me!" Shirez glared at the group of scouts. "Do you understand your orders?"

"Yes!" the largest scout spoke up. "We shall return with the boy and bring him directly to you."

Shirez dismissed the scouts and sat down on the king's throne. Looking around at the other members of the court who were watching him, Shirez proclaimed, "The king asked me to wait at his throne for the return of the scouts. He also asked for absolute silence from his court of idiots!"

The other attendants of the king bowed before Shirez and kept silent as requested.

7

FLASHDARK

"I t's me," Guardian said. "I am glad to see you ready and willing to begin our journey. "How do you like the sword so far?"

"This thing is amazing!" Charlie replied. "I was able to remove the seeds of deception and the roots! I even chopped them up into little tiny pieces until they turned to dust."

"Very well," Guardian answered.

Charlie picked up the sword and held it up against the blackness. "Guardian, what gives the sword its power?"

"It is the Sword of Truth," Guardian explained. "The truth is the power."

"How can the truth have power to light the darkness? I don't understand how that works," Charlie said, as he waved the sword out in front of him. "Can you explain it to me?"

"Yes, Charlie, you have asked an excellent question," Guardian agreed. "In the Bible, there are many verses that refer to God's Word as light or a lamp. God's word is truth. When you are faced with the darkness of the enemy, you really see the power of truth, because it is such a contrast to the darkness."

"I still don't get it," Charlie said, putting the sword next to his side. "This light and dark thing has me a bit confused."

"Okay, Charlie," Guardian continued. "Think of a shadow. A shadow is created by the light that shines around it. A shadow would not exist, except that it is the area that the light does not hit. A shadow is darkness. Now you might carry a flashlight to help you see in the darkness, so you know that darkness can be lit up by light. Can you carry a flashdark?"

"A what?" Charlie questioned.

"A flashdark," Guardian stated. "The opposite of a flashlight."

"There is no such thing as a flashdark," Charlie said.

"Think of a dark room with no light," Guardian said. "If you crack open a door or window to let in some light, the light invades the room and makes an enormous difference. All of a sudden, you would be able to see. Now try that in a room full of light and try to let in the darkness by opening a door or window. It just doesn't have the same effect, does it?"

"You are really smart," Charlie complimented the large angel. "Will this sword light up more than just the area in front of me?"

"The truth is what gives the power to the sword. Please remember that," Guardian insisted. "Truth is available in many forms from God. His truth is everywhere, once you know how to recognize it! The most important place to discover God's truth is the Bible. It is a far more powerful thing to know God's Word than to wave a sword around in front of you. Truth is power, God's power."

"Can we go find some truth?" Charlie asked.

"Let the journey begin!" Guardian shouted, as he and the boy walked along the path of light, using their Swords of Truth to light the edges of the trail. "Our first stop will be the river and then just beyond that is the Vault of Prayers."

As the two carefully made their way down the path, Charlie began to notice that the air was getting thick and heavy. The path beneath his feet began to darken and have some very slippery patches that made it feel as if he would lose his footing at any minute. "Guardian, what happened to the trail of light?"

"Do you remember that field Ol' Tie showed you?" Guardian questioned.

"Yes, what does that field have to do with this trail?" Charlie asked.

"Ol' Tie was growing snares and seeds of deceit in that field. The seeds he grows are planted, and the snares are intended to cover the light, trip us up, and slow our progress." Guardian said stopping for a moment. "But watch this!" Guardian found a snare and lifted it up with the tip of his sword. Dark sinewy roots hung off the snare, and underneath was a brightly lit stone. "See how the snare hides the light?" Then with one fluid movement, the angel flipped the snare into the air and sliced through it causing a fiery explosion. Debris rained down upon the trail, but the light increased, causing even the debris to disappear.

Amazed, Charlie continued on the trail, stopping every time he found a snare and following Guardian's example by destroying it and making the trail shine brighter.

Guardian stopped for a moment, turned to Charlie, and said in a somber voice, "It is important to keep the trail of light as clear as we can for the others who follow us."

Charlie laughed. "I don't know if anyone will ever travel this way again, but it is fun to expose and destroy!" Then he stopped for a minute, holding up the sword in front of him. He could see dark vines hanging from the trees. Fiery red eyes peered out from the heavy underbrush.

"Guardian?" Charlie called. "Whose eyes are those?"

"The King of Lies has sent scouts to find you and report back to him," Guardian answered. "Watch this!" Guardian held his sword near to the ground and spun around quickly causing red fiery eyes to shoot out into the darkness of the path. "There! That should limit their vision for a while."

"Amazing!" Charlie exclaimed. He then grasped his sword with both hands and swung low, hoping to cut off more of the prying eyes. "Take that!"

"Charlie!" Guardian yelled, as he watched the boy slip and fall his sword flying into the air above him, looking like it would fall down and pin the boy himself. "You must be more careful," Guardian said as he caught the sword, bringing it down gently next to Charlie. Guardian reached over to help Charlie up. Examining him with his own sword, he made sure that no debris from the demons had attached themselves to him.

Both Charlie's pride and back hurt, but he did not want to let Guardian know how much. "Guardian, do you remember when you said this Sword of Truth is only one of the pieces of my armor? Can you tell me about the others?"

"Yes, there are others," Guardian said. And then he whispered, "We need to stop for a moment. We have more company," Guardian stated. "Stay here. I shall destroy the demon and be right back."

"Okay," Charlie said, as he waved the sword more carefully in front of him. "I'll be right here."

Guardian slipped into the darkness, and Charlie stood alone for a moment. He really wanted to find out what the other pieces of armor were. He had read stories of knights wearing helmets and carrying shields to battles on horseback. He wondered if he would get some armor like that. A deep rumbling pierced his thoughts. "Thunder? Is that just thunder?" Charlie questioned himself, thinking a little bad weather would be nothing compared to what he had been facing. Charlie listened as the claps of thunder came closer. He had waited for what seemed an eternity, and then he heard a voice.

"Oh, good, I'm glad I found you!" a handsome young man approached Charlie. "Guardian said I would be able to find you here. I need to get you somewhere safe. There is a storm approaching."

8

THE BELT OF TRUTH

"You know Guardian?" Charlie questioned. "Where is he? Is he ok?"

"Oh, yeah. He just had some other things to attend to," the man said, rubbing his chin then taking off his cowboy hat and running his fingers through his thick hair. He continued, "He asked if I could help lead you down the path to a place where you can wait out the storm in safety. Would that be all right?"

Charlie lifted up the sword to study the man's face. He was tan and weathered, but before Charlie could get a real good look, the man took a step back into the darkness.

"You need to be careful with that thing. You don't want to poke someone's eye out!" he said.

"I'm sorry," Charlie said, lowering the sword and remembering that Guardian had also told him he needed to be careful with the sword. "I'll keep it down here at my side."

"Can I see the sword?" a second voice said as another cowboy-looking man approached from the blackness. "I've never seen a sword like that before."

Charlie looked at the new man standing near him and said, "I'm not sure Guardian would like it if I let someone else handle my sword." The men looked so much alike that Charlie asked, "Are you brothers?"

"Yes, we are brothers," a third voice answered as he walked toward Charlie. "But we are also good friends! Just like Guardian is a good friend of all of us! I am sure Guardian would not mind at all if we held that spectacular sword!"

Charlie held up the sword again to get a better look at the faces that were talking to him, but again, they moved back into the shadows, saying they did not want to get cut by a careless boy with a sword. "You know, I think I'll just hang on to it for now."

A huge crack of thunder pierced the air, and Charlie ducked a little as a fourth voice entered the trail. This time, the sound was of an older woman. "Oh, that's too bad! I know my sons would really enjoy looking at an exquisite piece of armor like that."

Charlie looked over at the woman. In her hands, she held a basket that was giving off a most wonderful aroma. "What's in there?" Charlie asked. "Whatever it is, it smells so good."

The woman replied, "Yes, this is very special food. This food had the important qualities of strength and perseverance. Guardian asked me to bring it to the shelter for you, as we wait out the storm together," the woman said with just a hint of cackle in her voice.

"Follow us! One of the cowboys said, and the three men and the one older woman began walking away from Charlie down the trail.

Another crack of thunder shook the ground and echoed overhead. As Charlie hit the ground for protection, he found himself at the place of decision again. *They say Guardian sent them, but I have been lied to before. The aroma is tempting and I am hungry, but I have been tempted before. Guardian told me to stay, but they want me to go.* Charlie held up the sword to light the darkness and prayed, "Please, God, help me to know what to do. Please help Guardian to find me!"

The four scouts continued down the trail for a bit before finally stopping to wait and listen for Charlie.

"Can you hear him?" the old woman asked.

"No, he is not following. How can he resist?" one cowboy said.

"Doesn't he need shelter?" another cowboy questioned.

"And food?" the third one said.

"Oh, Guardian! I am so glad to see you!" Charlie said, as he saw the enormous angel returning to the spot where he had been waiting.

"Are you alone?" Guardian asked.

"Now I am," Charlie explained. "There was a woman and three men that looked like cowboys. They told me that *you* had sent them to help me find shelter from the storm. They told me to follow them."

"Yet you did not follow them, I see," Guardian said, his smile growing wide across his face.

"I've been lied to and tempted before," Charlie said. "But I have to tell you that whatever that woman had in the basket sure smelled delicious!"

"Charlie, you are learning that many of the temptations of the world are just common things that we encounter daily. I'm very proud of you! You are learning to test people and situations. Some people never learn that. I think it is time to give you another piece of armor!"

"What?" Charlie asked excitedly.

Guardian lifted up one of his huge wings and pulled out a sparkling white belt. It was wide with a row of beautiful stones set into it. The buckle was made up of intricately carved solid gold.

"It's beautiful!" Charlie said. "Is it really mine?"

"Yes, Charlie. It is the Belt of Truth," Guardian said.

"Truth…truth! Oh no! Guardian!" Charlie said as he frantically searched his pockets. "I've lost the key of truth!"

Guardian smiled, as he reached under his wing again and pulled out the key. He carefully hooked it to the belt buckle and said, "There, now you won't lose it again."

"I'm so sorry!" Charlie said.

Handing the belt to Charlie, Guardian asked, "Why don't you try on the Belt of Truth?"

Charlie took the belt and wrapped it around his small frame. It was the most handsome belt he had ever seen. After making sure it fit just right, Charlie asked, "Should I keep this on all the time?"

"Yes," Guardian said. "The Belt of Truth is central to your character as a Christian. It is your stance. God, through his Word, has asked us to equip ourselves with the Belt of Truth in order to take our stand against the enemy. All that means is to be well-informed in what is true, so that we are able to recognize the subtle and not so subtle lies of the enemy."

Charlie adjusted the belt and stood up tall. "It makes me seem taller!"

Guardian smiled as he said, "Yes! You are standing tall and well-postured! You were able to recognize the enemy's lies and temptations!"

"Thank you, Guardian!" Charlie said.

One of the scouts finally broke the silence. "I don't think the kid is following us. We should let Shirez know."

"What?" the woman said. "Do you want to be cast into the abyss? No! We will find another way!"

The scouts began discussing how they would trap the boy and deliver him back to Shirez.

"Brilliant!" one scout said.

"Get rid of both of them at once!" another scout said.

The woman motioned to all the scouts and said, "Come with me. To capture the boy and destroy the angel, we need to reach the cave before they do. It is the only place that they can seek shelter from this storm."

9

THE HELMET

THUNDER RUMBLED IN the air, getting more intense with each passing wave.

"Do you think it will rain?" Charlie asked Guardian, as they continued walking down the path of light.

"It may," Guardian stated. "We need to find some shelter before that happens."

"Oh, I don't mind a little water," Charlie said.

"Water would be fine with me too. But the rain here is wicked," Guardian stated.

"Like super heavy?"

"No, more like burning coals and streams of hot acid."

Charlie stopped, as another clap of thunder shook the ground. "Where is the nearest shelter?" he asked anxiously.

"There is a cave just around that group of vines up there. We can wait out the storm in there," Guardian answered.

Guardian was right. Beyond the tangle of vines, there was a cave. It could not be seen from the trail, but Guardian cleared the way and ducked his enormous frame into the entry. Charlie followed, squeezing into the extra space underneath his wings.

"Sure is dark in here," Charlie said. As soon as the words left his mouth, he had an idea and began to sing a praise song. He delighted with how every word of thanksgiving lit up the air. Soon, Guardian chimed in, and the two sang in beautiful harmony. When the song ended, Charlie said, "Angels sure have good voices!"

"Well, thank you," Guardian said. "We get a lot of practice."

Suddenly, the cave walls shook and rocks began to tumble down, threatening to bury the entrance and trap them inside.

Guardian motioned to Charlie to be quiet and then whispered, "We need to go."

"But Guardian," Charlie whispered back. "What about the storm? Remember, burning coals and acid?"

"We will be protected by our helmets," Guardian answered, as he struggled to pull two helmets from under his wings in the cramped quarters. He put the larger one on his own head and then handed the smaller one to Charlie. "Go ahead and try it on."

"My own helmet too? Cool!" Charlie strapped the helmet on his head. Then he pulled up his belt, checking to make sure he had the key of truth still with him, raised his sword, and said, "Let's go!"

Guardian moved out cautiously from the cave constantly looking behind him to make sure Charlie was close. "Charlie, I know it's very dark. Are you okay? Use your sword if you think you are going to trip. Charlie?" Turning around and raising his own sword, Guardian could see that the figure behind him that he thought was Charlie was actually one of the enemy's scouts. "What have you done with the boy?"

"He is gone!" taunted the scout. "All gone!"

Stepping aside, the mighty angel commanded, "Show yourself!"

The vines that grew next to the cave started shaking. From their roots grew demon after demon, surrounding the mighty warrior. Guardian looked up, "Lord, may your power and presence prevail. Please strengthen me for the battle!" Guardian reached out with his sword and made a circle all about him. "I stand here in authority of the most High and by His power."

Suddenly, Guardian felt one of the roots grab his foot. Pulling hard, the root struggled to cause the mighty warrior to fall. Quickly, Guardian reached down with his sword and sliced the root off, tossing the debris into the outer darkness. Looking up, a set of fiery eyes descended upon Guardian's head, trying to pierce and burn through his helmet. Guardian grabbed the fire and crushed it in his mighty hand. Another demon came at him from the left with ropes of fear and bondage. Guardian, once again, wielded his sword and shredded the ropes into many pieces. Taking a deep breath, he blew the remnants into the darkness. Several demons surrounded the mighty Guardian, yet he continued to fight back with his sword, calling upon the name of the Lord, and defeating the demons.

Then Guardian called out to the last demon standing, "Bring yourself out of the shadows, so I may slay you also!" But all Guardian could hear was the rustle of the brush, as the demon ran away. Turning, Guardian quickly made his way back to the last place he had seen Charlie.

Charlie raised his head slowly off the ground. "What happened?" he said, trying to clear his thoughts. The last thing he remembered was walking behind Guardian and then, all of a sudden, there was no ground, no trail. The enemy must have built a pit within the trail. Quickly assessing himself, Charlie took inventory. "Helmet, belt, sword, and key. No broken bones. I seem okay." Charlie held out his sword to see where he was and saw the face of the old woman from earlier.

"I brought you the food you need," she cackled.

"I don't want your food, "Charlie said, holding up the sword and forcing her to back away from him. "Where is Guardian?"

"Dead," the woman responded.

"Well," Charlie said, "that means he is alive! Because all you do is lie!"

The woman growled and hissed at Charlie. Her form changed from an elderly woman to a hideous demon. "What is your name?" the creature demanded of Charlie.

"What is yours?" Charlie countered.

"Away with you!" the demon screamed, as it lunged at Charlie.

Charlie stood firm. Holding his sword directly at the demon, he said, "In the name of Jesus, I defeat you! Your lies and your evil must leave this place!"

The demon ran full speed on into the sword and exploded into smoke, which dissipated quickly into the night. Charlie was thrown back against the pit wall but was quickly able to regain his footing. Checking to make sure he had all of his armor, he began to sing a praise song to light the air. Finding a vine hanging down into the pit, he scaled the wall and scrambled up to the top just in time to see Guardian walking away.

"Hey! Where have you been?" Charlie said with a wry smile. "Have you been goofing off while I have been busy slaying the enemy?"

Guardian shook his head and raised his sword. The two touched swords and powerful sparks ignited the night. "Now to the Vault of Prayers, my warrior friend!"

10

THE BOOTS

CHARLIE LOST SIGHT of Guardian, as he struggled to keep up with the angel. Finally, he saw a river. Looking up and down the shoreline, he called out, "Is there a bridge somewhere?" Charlie looked around. "Guardian? Hey, Guardian! I said is there a bridge?" Charlie called out, but his words were met with empty echoes in the night. "Must be slaying another demon," Charlie muttered to himself.

Then he walked carefully to the river's edge. The forest floor dipped slightly to make room for the water's flow. A wide expanse of water with a calm current was churning below. The marks on the bank made it clear that the water level had been much higher recently, but looking up and down the bank now, Charlie only sensed a peace in the soothing sounds that lulled him. Kneeling and placing his fingers against the flow, he enjoyed the refreshingly cool water wash over his dirty and scraped-up hands. Sitting down, he took off his dirty shoes and socks then rolling up his jeans, he dipped his feet in the river. The water was cold at first, but his feet seemed to acclimate quickly to the water. This was a place where Charlie felt time had slowed down. He turned so his head could rest upon the shore while the water still caressed his feet, and he began to doze.

A sharp noise brought Charlie out of his sleepy state.

"Charlie! Get up, quickly! We must cross the river now!" Guardian called out as he ran straight into the river.

"Guardian?" Charlie tried to wake himself up and understand what was going on. "Okay, just let me put my shoes back on."

"No time!" Guardian said, as he reached back and whisked Charlie up from the shore.

"Are you sure? It looks deep and the water was calm, but now it is moving pretty fast!" Charlie did not want to admit what a poor swimmer he was.

"Follow me," Guardian said, as he stepped into the swiftly moving water. "The river will only get deeper and stronger the more you wait. We must cross now!"

Charlie looked around hoping a bridge would magically appear. He realized that he was not going to get out of crossing the water, and he would do better to stay close to Guardian. Slowly, he stepped into the rushing water and felt his feet immediately swallowed up by the river's sandy bottom. "Help, Guardian!"

"Keep moving, Charlie. Follow me to the other side."

"Guardian! I'm getting stuck!" Charlie cried out. "I don't know if I can make it to the other side!"

"Follow me, Charlie," Guardian's voice barely audible against the roar of the water.

Fine! Easy for an enormous angel to cross a river. Charlie trudged, carefully lifting each of his feet out of the mud with a deep sucking sound and then placing them in front of him. Fighting the current that pushed against his legs, he leaned toward the other side of the river. After several steps, he felt the sand must be getting thinner as his steps felt more solid. Finally, upon reaching the other side, he climbed up onto the river's shore. Exhausted, Charlie plopped himself down on the bare ground.

Looking down at his soaking wet clothes, he said, "What was all that about? Why the big rush? Now I'm soaking wet…my—my feet! Look at my feet!"

A golden sheen encased Charlie's feet like tall boots, but the sole was solid gold and the heel was of purple stone. Adorning both sides were various stones along with ornate stitching in a glistening white thread that stood out in contrast to the golden background. "I've always wanted cowboy boots!" Charlie exclaimed. "The river did this! Can I keep them?"

"Charlie, I will explain later, but for now, we must continue on," Guardian said motioning to the dark cave just ahead of them.

"Can't we rest for just a minute?" Charlie asked as he reluctantly got up.

Guardian did not seem to notice Charlie's hesitation as he pointed toward the cave. Guardian began to climb the rock face. His massive form making quick work of the sheer slope that led to the cave entrance.

Charlie struggled to keep up but noticed that his new boots had incredible traction. As he trusted them to grip the terrain, he found that he could scale places that he never thought he would be able to, feeling stronger and more agile than ever before.

"Do you like them?" Guardian asked as he looked back. "Your feet have been shod in the Gospel of Peace."

"The gospel? Like the Bible?"

"They are part of the armor. Your point of contact with this world is your feet. You need to approach your life making sure that the Word of God is at the center of your contact with the world," Guardian explained.

"Wow! These are so cool! Do they do something? Do they have power?" Charlie asked.

"Does the armor of God have power? I think you know and have seen that it does." Guardian continued. "I want you to remember that the Word of the God goes with you everywhere. The Word can lead and guide you."

Charlie did not really understand what Guardian was talking about, but he loved his new boots. Looking up into the massive rock face, Charlie notice a door imbedded within the rock. "Does that door lead to the Vault of Prayers?"

"Yes, Charlie, follow me," Guardian said

Guardian approached the old wooden door and held his sword in the air as if he was looking around for someone, then he whispered, "Do you still have the key?"

"Yes." Charlie lifted the key off his belt and held it up.

"Go ahead." Guardian motioned for Charlie to unlock the door.

Charlie placed the key in the lock, slowly turning it until he heard the click. Light flooded the area where they stood, filling the night as the door swung open slowly. Charlie stepped into the passageway just beyond the door and was overcome with the most pleasant aroma. "Oh, Guardian, it's beautiful!"

11

THE VAULT

GUARDIAN ENTERED BEHIND Charlie and drew a deep breath. "Ah," he said, as he bolted the door closed behind them. "Do you like it?"

Charlie looked around in amazement upon seeing the piles and stacks of golden bricks that surrounded them. "We've found treasure!" Charlie exclaimed.

"Treasure, yes, and wisdom also," Guardian said, as he handed one of the bricks to Charlie. "Go ahead and place it next to your ear."

"My ear?" Charlie questioned, as he took the brick and was caught off guard by its weight. "Gold is heavy!"

"Listen, Charlie, listen," Guardian said patiently.

Charlie used both hands to hold the brick and did not hear anything at first. Then he pressed the brick to his ear and began to make out a familiar voice. *"Now I lay me down to sleep, pray the Lord my soul to keep. If I die before I wake, pray the Lord my soul to take. Please bless Mommy and Daddy, amen."*

Charlie pulled the brick away from his ear and exclaimed, "That's my voice! That's me! How did you do that, Guardian?"

"It is not my doing," Guardian said. "It's your doing."

"I didn't do it," Charlie protested. "It's my voice, but I didn't put it inside a brick of gold!"

"You are correct," Guardian said. "Your heavenly Father is the one who keeps the prayers."

Charlie stood in disbelief. After a few moments, he walked over and grabbed another golden brick and held it to his ear, *"Please God help me to get better. I hate having chickenpox! Please make me better!"* Confused, Charlie dropped the brick. "That's me! It really is me!"

Guardian handed another brick to Charlie. Excitedly, Charlie held this one up to his ear. *"Father, my time is almost done here on earth. I ask, in the name of Jesus, if you are willing please pour out your Spirit upon my descendants. Keep each child and grandchild of mine under the power of your gaze. Teach them your ways through your Holy Spirit. I pray, if you are willing, I will meet each one of them in the kingdom as we spend eternal life together. I ask these things in the precious name of your son, Jesus. Amen."*

"That's my grandma!" Charlie said. "She passed away about two years ago. But here she is praying. God keeps these? He really keeps all these prayers, even after people are gone?"

"Gone?" Guardian questioned. "What do you mean gone?"

"You know what I mean…I mean dead. I went to her funeral. How can this be her voice?" Charlie asked.

"Your grandmother loved to dance, didn't she?" Guardian asked.

"Yes, she would tell us stories of how she and Papa met on the dance floor and then spent the next sixty years of marriage dancing together," Charlie said. "Grandma was so sad when Papa died. Sometimes I would catch her dancing in the kitchen, like she was still dancing with him. She never knew I saw her."

"Yes, they have a standing Saturday night date," Guardian said. "They are such a lovely couple to watch!"

"What do you mean?" Charlie asked. "They are both dead!"

"They have passed on from this world—the earthly world," Guardian explained. "However, they are eternally alive in heaven. I've met both of them several times. They talk about you and your sister, Sarah all the time. I felt like I already knew you before we even met!"

Charlie sat in the Vault of Prayers, totally overwhelmed, talking about the dead as if they were alive and listening to prayers from the past. He finally asked, "Did my grandmother's prayer have anything to do with me being here?"

"Yes, she is quite the prayer warrior! Her prayers live on, because prayer has power. She lives on, because she has eternal life!" Guardian said, as he handed Charlie another brick, "Here, listen to this one."

Charlie held the brick close to his ear and listened intently. At first, the words were just a whisper, then they grew stronger with each breath. *"Help me, God! I don't know how to do this! I don't know how to be the father I need to be!"*

"That's my dad!" Charlie whispered. "My dad is praying. He is asking God for help."

"Yes, Charlie," Guardian said in a very somber tone, as he handed yet another brick to Charlie. "Your dad needs help. Here listen to this one."

"Dear Lord, I am so sorry. I know divorce is wrong, but we are struggling. Is it better to always have the kids see us fight? Please help me!"

"That's my dad again," Charlie said. "They used to fight a lot!"

Guardian motioned to two piles of bricks within the vault. "Take all the time you need."

Charlie spent what felt like hours going through the two piles. The pile on the right was prayers from his mom.

That pile was much larger than the one on the left, which belonged to his dad. But each pile was filled with the voices of his parents, crying out for help. Each one was confused with how their marriage fell apart and came to the point of considering a divorce, each one searching for answers.

"Guardian," Charlie began, "I never knew my dad even believed in God. I never knew he would ask for help. I've hated my dad for so long, because he left my mom. I've hated my mom for letting him leave. My mom and dad are both asking for help!" Charlie's face glistened with tears. "I didn't know!"

Guardian moved closer to the boy, wrapping one wing over his shoulder, and whispered, "It's okay, Charlie."

Charlie pushed away from the angel, "But, Guardian, you don't understand! I've been angry for so long! I even wanted to get even! That is why I am running away, to hurt them!" Charlie fell down on his knees. "You don't understand how ugly I am on the inside!"

"Let me ask you a question, Charlie. Are you ready to forgive your parents?" Guardian waited patiently as Charlie searched his own emotions.

"I want to, Guardian. I want to be able to forgive them. I just feel so ugly on the inside. Do you know what I mean?"

"Yes, I do know what you mean. You are free to ask God to forgive you. But let me explain something about forgiveness. It's a two-way street. If you ask your heavenly Father to forgive you yet you harbor unforgiveness in your heart against someone else, you will not experience the freedom from release."

"What do you mean *freedom from release*?" Charlie asked.

"It is the forgiveness process I am speaking about. It is something you can use your heart-eyes to see," Guardian explained.

"My heart-eyes? What do you mean, Guardian? I remember you said something about using my heart-eyes earlier."

"It is what you have been in training to do on this journey, Charlie, to see the spiritual realm with the eyes of your heart—your heart-eyes."

"Guardian, what do I do? Please just tell me what to do!" Charlie said, crumpling to the ground.

"What do you think the first step is?"

"I guess I need to ask God to forgive me."

"Yes, exactly! What is next?" Guardian asked excitedly.

"I—I need to ask God to help me to forgive my parents!" Charlie said.

"Yes! Then do you know what will happen?"

"The forgiveness process?" Charlie asked hesitantly.

"Yes, you have it!" Guardian said. "Now close your physical eyes and watch the process with your heart-eyes!"

Charlie closed his physical eyes and opened his heart-eyes. Suddenly, he saw Jesus standing before him. "Jesus, is that really you?"

"Yes, Charlie, it's really me," Jesus replied.

Charlie reached out, as Jesus took his hands and lifted him up. "I need to ask you for forgiveness," Charlie said as he began to cry. "I've been mean and angry and just so ugly on the inside. Can God forgive me for being mad at my mom and dad? I'm so sorry. I never thought that they might have problems and just need help. I thought they didn't care about me and Sarah."

Jesus listened patiently, all the while gently wiping the tears from Charlie's face. When Charlie was finished, Jesus reached out and gently lifted Charlie's chin saying, "Charlie, I gave my life for this very reason, so that you could live a life free from the burdens and wounds of the enemy." Jesus reached toward Charlie's heart and took the tear-soaked cloth and began gently washing it until every speck of unforgiveness and every dark stain was gone.

"Will God forgive me?" Charlie asked.

"Consider it done," Jesus replied.

"I feel clean!" Charlie said. "I feel…I just feel good! Thank you!"

"Unforgiveness is such a dirty thing. I hate it," Jesus said.

"How does it happen, Jesus?" Charlie asked. "How did my heart get so stained?"

"The enemy has many weapons in his arsenal: bitterness, jealousy, resentment, and arrogance, just to name a few. These things take root upon your heart causing it to darken, and they leave a stain"

"Oh, yeah! I've had experience with the roots of arrogance. That was awful!" Charlie said.

"How do you feel now?"

"I feel really good! Thank you!"

"Good. I have a gift for you."

"A gift? Cool!"

Jesus raised his hand, and a beautiful shield suddenly appeared in it. Jesus turned the front of the shield toward his own eyes and exclaimed, Exquisite!"

"Let me see," Charlie said excitedly.

Jesus turned the shield toward Charlie, as the boy guarded his eyes from the brightness. "Do you like it?"

"It's so bright!" Charlie exclaimed.

"Here," Jesus said, handing Charlie the shield. "Go ahead and hold it."

Charlie grabbed the handle, as Jesus released it into the boy's small hands. "Does this thing have a motor or batteries or something?" Charlie asked. "I can feel power pulsating from it."

"Faith has a power of its own, no batteries needed." Jesus chuckled.

Charlie looked closely at the front of the shield. The entire face was covered in broken pieces of glass. Blues, greens, reds, and purples, too. Every color imaginable. "Jesus, why is the shield made of broken pieces?"

"Good question, Charlie! Each piece represents a time in your life when you struggled or doubted, yet you chose to have faith in God. When you choose to believe that God works all things for the good of those who are called according to his purpose, you make a beautiful faith." Jesus said, as a smile spread across his face.

Charlie studied the shield for a moment. "Seems to me the more broken the pieces, the more beautiful the faith. But I have not lived long enough to make this many decisions. There are hundreds of broken pieces here."

"Yes," Jesus said. "Your heavenly Father sees you as you are: past, present, and future. He is omnipresent."

"Omni what?"

"Let's just say, your heavenly Father sees the big picture."

"Okay, I get that." Charlie was satisfied with the answer.

Suddenly, the shield began to pulse and shake in Charlie's hands. "Uh…Jesus, it seems like the shield wants to do something!" Charlie tried to keep it under control. "What should I do?"

Jesus smiled as he said, "I believe we are in for a demonstration of what faith can do! Did you know that faith can extinguish any flaming missile, any fiery dart of the evil one?"

"That's a verse from the Bible!" Charlie said.

"Yes, the very Word of God!" Jesus said. "Now hold out your shield."

Just as Jesus spoke, a great darkness came upon them. It covered them completely.

"What do I do Jesus?" Charlie shouted.

"Hold on to your faith!" Jesus proclaimed, as light-filled streams shot out of the shield, shattering the darkness. Then from the side, flaming missiles began shooting at the shield. Charlie turned the shield just in time and watched as faith extinguished each one. The darkness and missiles fell to the ground like debris from a campfire before evaporating into the air. "Faith can be both defensive and offensive," Jesus added.

"Like teams in football?" Charlie asked.

"Yes, just like in football," Jesus answered. "Would like you to see the offensive now?"

"Yes, please," Charlie said. "This thing is crazy!"

"Watch what happens when you allow faith to reach out and go into the world!" Jesus took the shield from Charlie's hands and placed it firmly on the ground. Charlie watched in wonder as hundreds of roots shot out from the bottom of the shield. Root after root crept out, until it began breaking up the ground before it. Then in one seamless motion, Jesus waved his hand over the rough ground. Golden seeds fell into the open rows. Then with another wave of his hand, he produced water flowing into each of the newly formed rows. After that, the ground shook, and out of it came blossoming flowers with the most fragrant smell.

"You made a garden!" Charlie exclaimed.

"This is the gift of faith," Jesus said. "Your faith can break up the fallow ground and make a way for the seeds of truth to be planted. The seeds can then grow and blossom. Then the air will be filled with hope—the aroma of Christ!

"You do smell so good," Charlie said as he closed his eyes.

Jesus whispered, "It is time for you to open your physical eyes now, Charlie. There is much work for us to do."

Charlie opened his eyes, looking around for Jesus but found himself still sitting with Guardian in the vault of prayers. "Guardian, I'm forgiven! And I've got a shield of faith!"

Guardian smiled. "Looks like it is time for us to plant some seeds."

12

OUR HERITAGE

SHIREZ SAT IMPATIENTLY on the king's throne, awaiting news from the scouts he had sent out to capture the boy. Finally, a single shadowy figure approached the throne.

"My Lord," he growled, as he placed a black bag at the feet of Shirez. "I have brought you the boy as you commanded."

"Show me!" demanded Shirez. He reached down, ready to cut open the black sack himself.

The scout approached Shirez, bowing low. "Allow me, my lord." With one quick motion, the demon ripped the cord that held the top closed, and its demonic contents fell to the floor.

"Ecnagorra!" Shirez gasped. "I thought the king had you killed!"

"Fool!" Ecnagorra shrieked. "No one can defeat my plans! I will rule this kingdom!"

Ecnagorra scrambled to his feet and quickly summoned his cohorts. As they bound Shirez, they tried to decide who they would pledge their allegiance to.

Drawn by the commotion, the King of Lies entered his court. "Ecnagorra! Prepare yourself for the abyss! You will surely die this time!" Turning to his attendants, the king demanded, "Seize the traitor!"

Shirez wrestled free from his captors and stood between the king and Ecnagorra. "It is I who will rule this kingdom," Shirez shouted. "Any king that is referring to the scriptures of the light is not fit to rule!"

From behind the throne, four mighty demons reached out to protect the king. Ecnagorra rose to his full stature and incinerated them in one swift flaming attack.

Realizing the power of his adversary, Shirez immediately turned and subdued the king with chains of bondage. Mentally planning the demise of his foe, he hissed to Ecnagorra, "Perhaps we can rule together!"

Ecnagorra glared at the formidable demon, Shirez. Weighing his options, he decided to play along for the moment. "Tell me, what advantage will I gain by allowing you to live?"

Shirez quickly responded, "Do you not understand the best way to capture the boy?"

"Tell me more of your plan," Ecnagorra said, studying his opponent closely. "What do you have in mind?"

Shirez began, "We need bait that the boy cannot refuse."

"What bait will allow us to capture the boy?" Ecnagorra demanded. "We have tempted him with food and shelter. The boy does not believe our lies!" Ecnagorra's spit sizzled on the floor as he shouted.

Shirez hissed, "We will offer him the things of his world that are most desirable: wealth, power, and happiness!"

Ecnagorra kicked the bound king away from the throne, as he took his seat. "Tell me more."

Shirez laid out his plan of deception before the mighty Ecnagorra. They both agreed to a truce for the time being, as they commanded the remaining court assistants to throw the king into the dungeon. "We will surely capture the boy this time!" Shirez screamed.

Ecnagorra answered with a hideous laugh. "Yes, he will have no way to refuse us now."

Guardian and Charlie left the vault of prayers and crossed the river in no time. They began their travels by following the path of light that led into the distance on an upward trail.

Charlie stopped for a moment, as he adjusted his belt. "Tell me, Guardian, what do the stones represent? I see the same four stones imbedded on each piece of armor and even within the key of truth."

"Great question," Guardian responded. "The stones are precious in that they remind us of our heritage."

"Our heritage? What do you mean?"

Guardian pointed to the stones on Charlie's boots. "See here, the first stone. This is a diamond. Do you know how diamonds are formed?"

"Uh, sorry. I don't think we have covered that in school yet."

"Diamonds are known to be one of the hardest natural materials that ever existed. They are formed at great depths within the earth through pressure and intense heat. Then they are forced to the surface by volcanic activity," Guardian explained.

"I still don't get it."

"The diamonds represent your faith, Charlie. Your faith is formed under pressure, during the trials and difficulties of your life."

"Oh, yeah. Jesus and I talked about how faith is formed."

Guardian then pointed to the next gem. "Do you recognize this one?"

"All I can tell you is that it is purple and really very pretty. My mom has a necklace with that stone," Charlie said.

"This is amethyst," Guardian said. "This stone is considered to be the color of royalty in your world. The warriors of old believed that if they wore this gem into battle, it would provide them protection from the enemy."

"Really? Just by wearing a stone?"

"Charlie," Guardian continued. "When you read your history, you will see that many things in your world, your civilization, have been deemed to possess supernatural powers to heal and to defend. Yet you will find only one thing has the power to deliver you from the forces of evil, and that is the Living God and his Word, the Bible."

"I've seen that power in action!" Charlie exclaimed, as he waved his sword through the air.

"Careful!" Guardian ducked out of the way. "Now the next stone you see here is called jasper."

"Jasper? Never heard of it!" Charlie reluctantly laid his sword next to his side.

"One form of Jasper is called a bloodstone. Do you see the red marks within the stone? There is a legend in your world that says it was the stone Christ's blood dripped on as he hung from the cross."

"That's terrible!" Charlie gasped.

"Actually," Guardian continued, "that explanation helps to remind us of Christ's sacrifice for us. We are sanctified by the blood of Christ. It is very important that we never take Jesus's sacrifice for granted."

Charlie sat very quietly for a moment. "You know, I have learned this stuff in Sunday school, but it never seemed real to me. More like a story in an old book. But when you see the Word of God in action, when you watch faith change the landscape from ugly to beautiful and meet Jesus in person, then the whole story of the gospel makes sense!"

"Yes," Guardian said. "You have been given a special gift to be able to experience these things with your heart-eyes and the ability to see the spiritual things clearly."

"What is the last stone, Guardian? Is it blue because it is supposed to remind us that Jesus will return out of the sky someday? Or maybe that he walked on water?"

Guardian scratched his chin. "Well, no, that's not what I was going to say. But you know, I kind of like that! I think you have been given the gift of wisdom and insight along with faith!"

"What does it represent?" Charlie asked.

"The last stone is sapphire. In your world, some believe it to be the stone on which the Ten Commandments were written. The sapphire reminds us of the solid foundation of God's Word to us—the Bible."

"Thank you, Guardian, for taking the time to explain stuff like this to me." Charlie ran his fingers over the stones on his boots and stood up. "Now, what did you mean when you said it is time to plant some seeds?"

"Follow me." The large angel motioned up the trail. "I have just the field in mind to do some landscaping!"

13

THE SOWER

"My king!" Ecnagorra bowed low before the bound King in the dungeon. "I regret the treatment you have had to endure. Please pardon the ruse that we have had to go through to keep Shirez in the dark." Ecnagorra motioned for the guards to remove the bindings from the king. They approached warily, knowing full well they may be scorched and sent into the abyss themselves. "I hope you will be understanding of the depth of our plan to keep the Promise from being fulfilled."

The king shook off the last remaining chains of bondage and rose to his full height. The guards fell flat on their faces, as they begged for mercy. Ecnagorra even took a step back, fearing the worst.

"Understanding? Understanding? You ask for me to be tolerant of your lack of respect and treatment of me, your king?"

Ecnagorra mustered his pride and courage and approached the king. "My king," he said, bowing low before him. "I myself read the scriptures of the light, and I see that we indeed have the Promise upon us. I am grateful for your wisdom and knowledge to warn us of this devastating event."

Somewhat appeased, the King motioned for one of the assistants to get him a chair. As he sat, his eyes never left the face of Ecnagorra. He was studying the powerful demon. "So you understand the full consequence if the Promise is allowed to be fulfilled?"

"Yes, my king," Ecnagorra said, still bowing. "This child must be stopped!"

"What is your plan?" The king questioned eagerly.

Ecnagorra took a deep breath, as he explained to the king that there was evidence the boy had been to the vault of prayers and that, not only did he have the Sword of the Spirit, he also had other parts of the Armor of God. No one had been able to confirm exactly which pieces the boy was equipped with. "I believe that the plan of reaching the boy by offering him wealth, power, and happiness is a valid plan. If the boy is consumed with promoting himself, he will be vulnerable to us. We can then capture him, and he will work for us. He will have no choice."

"I like it," the king said as he stood up. Then breathing a shot of fire directly at Ecnagorra, he screamed, "And what of the wretched Shirez? How does he fit into this plan?"

Ecnagorra ducked and rolled away from the flames just in time. Quickly recovering, he stood up and faced the king. "Shirez will only be around as long as he is useful to our plan, not a moment longer, my king."

Guardian and Charlie approached a field along the trail.

"Guardian, that looks like the field that the old farmer showed me. Tieced was his name, but he said to call him Ol' Tie."

"Yes, I am familiar with Tieced," Guardian said.

Charlie continued. "He is the one who gave me the cookies with the seeds of deception in them. He said they were from this field!"

Guardian's face lit up. "Are you ready to use your shield?"

"Am I ever!"

Guardian moved over and helped to hold Charlie's hand steady on the shield. "Do you remember the power of faith that Jesus showed you?"

"Yes! Can we do that here?" Charlie reached out and held the shield with both his hands to steady it as it shook from the power rumbling within. "Am I in the right spot?"

Guardian knelt next to the shield and prayed. "Father, we pray that the landscape here would be changed from a field of deception and a place full of snares to a garden of growing faith and the aroma of Christ. We ask that this field would be a sign of hope and refreshment for any travelers that pass this way in the future."

As soon as Guardian had finished the prayer, Charlie's shield began shooting roots out from the bottom. Each one thrust forward with such power, it flipped every snare and tore every deception plant completely out of the ground—roots and all. As the plants flew into the air, they exploded and fell down as ashes on the field. The field that was once planted with darkness was now a field of freshly plowed soil.

"Cool!" Charlie shouted. I love this shield!"

"Yes, Faith is an amazing and powerful force!"

"Guardian, where do we get the seeds to plant in the garden. Jesus had them with him last time. Do you have some?"

"Watch," Guardian said, as he motioned for Charlie to move to the side of the field. The two sat quietly for a few moments, then Charlie finally saw a figure approach the field.

"She is beautiful!" Charlie said. "Hey, she has a Key of Truth hanging off her bag! Does she have seeds to plant in there?"

"Yes," Guardian said. "Her name is the Sower. She reflects well the heart of Christ, and the Maker trusts her with seeds to plant and grow faith. She has been given the gifts of both wisdom and prophecy. The Word is like food to her. She takes it in and is able to return it to the world in a way that grows hope, the aroma of Christ."

Charlie watched as the woman knelt and prayed. When she spoke out loud, her exquisite words—like a song—flew with the breeze. When she had finished praying, she reached into the bag and pulled out a handful of golden seeds. Standing back and looking up to heaven, she thanked God then threw the seeds forward. Each one landed into the row appointed for it. Suddenly, there was a shower of light and water, filling each row and covering all of the seeds. "Am I seeing with my heart-eyes right now?" Charlie asked.

"Excellent question," Guardian said. "Yes! Faith has the power to change even the dirtiest landscape to a place of hope!"

"What you're saying is, just because the enemy meant something for evil, it can be changed into something good by the power of God, right?" Charlie asked.

"Yes!" A wide smile filled the Guardian's face. "But I have a favor to ask of you. When you meet this woman again, will you please remind her how special she is to the kingdom of God?"

"Sure. You really think I will see her again?"

"Yes, you will," Guardian assured the boy.

"Look!" Charlie exclaimed. "The field! It's growing beautiful flowers!"

"Yes, the landscape is changing!" Guardian motioned to Charlie. "Come with me, the enemy will soon be here and will be furious at the loss of this field of deception and snares! They will begin to look for other ways to destroy and devastate."

"I'm not afraid of the enemy!" Charlie stated boldly.

"I am glad to hear that," Guardian said. "Wisdom is one of our best weapons. Being aware of the enemy's tactics and advances gives us the upper hand and the ability to gain the victory in the name of Jesus. But we don't need to go looking for trouble either."

"Okay," Charlie agreed reluctantly. "I just wanted to use my sword again."

"Until we are home, there will always be another battle to fight. But for now, please follow me," Guardian said, as he pointed up the trail.

14

SPLASH

SHIREZ SAT UPON the throne as Ecnagorra entered the court.

"Is the king disposed of?" Shirez asked.

Ecnagorra bent stiffly, acknowledging the question. "It is as you say."

"Now we must prepare for the completion of our plan!" Shirez motioned to several of the court assistants who stumbled over each other, trying to get to the throne first. "I need a room prepared for the boy, so he can be held captive and taught the ways of evil."

One of the scouts, who had been listening to the plans all evening, asked, "Will the room for the boy be temporary or permanent?"

"Fool!" hissed Shirez. "Permanent, of course!"

Charlie sat down next to a log and closed his eyes. "I've been practicing looking with my heart-eyes, Guardian."

"Good for you!" the enormous angel cheered. "What sorts of things have you been seeing?"

"Recently, and even right now, I see this shower of stuff falling down like rain, but it isn't rain. It's golden, kind of looks like glitter—but better. Mixed in with the gold, there are also super shiny pieces of purple, blue, green, and…oh, just a total rainbow of colors. This stuff just keeps pouring!"

"Charlie, you truly are seeing with the eyes of your heart!"

"But what is it, Guardian?"

Guardian smiled. "What you are seeing is the outpouring of the Holy Spirit in your life."

"Like the Promise?"

"Yes, Charlie," Guardian answered. "You are seeing the Promise fulfilled in your life."

Charlie smiled wide, as he kept his physical eyes closed and his heart-eyes open. "Should I do anything with all this stuff? Should I be catching it and putting it in containers to have it with me later?"

"Oh, no, quite the opposite, "Guardian replied. "You should do what Jesus did with it."

"What is that?"

"Jesus liked to splash people." Guardian said.

"How do I do that?" Charlie asked.

Guardian moved behind the boy and said, "Now I am going to lift you up and show you something." The mighty angel slipped his arms under the boy's arms and raised him to his feet. Then covering the boy's hands with his own, he held out their hands together, palms up.

"It's splashing everywhere!" Charlie exclaimed. "It is so beautiful! I can see the colors so perfectly now. Oh my! I'm splashing!"

"By lifting your hands, you are acknowledging the origin of the Promise of your heavenly Father. By allowing it to splash off your own hands, you share it with those around you."

"It seems so simple."

"But it is not simple," Guardian explained. "Remember, what you are seeing is spiritual not physical. What you see in the spiritual realm requires great discipline. You must remember that it still exists, even if it is unseen in the physical realm. Can you remember that at all times God is present with his Holy Spirit and he is pouring out his power and Promise upon you?"

"Yes!" Charlie answered.

"Then, my dear boy, you will be a great splasher!"

"Ecnagorra!" Shirez commanded. "Have you received a report on the progress of the boy?"

"Yes, my lord," Ecnagorra said, growling under his breath. "The boy is on his way to us as we speak."

"Now it is time," Guardian said. "You have been chosen to reach out to the lost. You have been chosen to receive the Promise and help strengthen the minds of those who are led astray by deception, fear, arrogance, and lies. You know how to fight, Charlie! You have been chosen to teach others."

Charlie bowed his head and thanked the Lord for taking care of him. Then he promised that he would do his best to be the person that the Lord wanted him to be. Charlie and the angel seemed to make it back to the top of the trail so quickly, almost as if they were flying.

"Go now, Charlie, and ask God how he is to use you for his kingdom."

"I will!" Charlie said, and he began walking. Turning to thank the mighty angel, he saw that Guardian was already gone.

"Don't go yet!" a voice called out. "You know you are missing a piece of armor, don't you?"

"Who is there?" Charlie called out as he searched the area. "Guardian, is that you?"

"My name is not Guardian, but I am an angel," the voice said.

"Show yourself!" Charlie demanded, raising his sword.

Immediately, an angel appeared before Charlie. He was dressed all in white, except the very tips of his wings were covered in soot. He was a small angel without any armor. "My name is Apollo," the angel said as he stepped toward Charlie. "I have been sent to give you your last piece of armor."

"Guardian never mentioned you," Charlie said warily. "How do I know you are who you say you are?"

"I see you have been given the gift of wisdom along with heart-eyes," Apollo said. "However, I do not need to prove my power nor my existence to you. I have been sent to make sure you receive your last piece of armor, the breastplate. If you choose to disregard this piece of armor, then that is your decision."

"What? I did not say I didn't want my armor!" Charlie protested. "The breastplate would complete my protection. Do you have it with you?"

"With me? Foolish child! Do you not understand the power and importance of this piece? Perhaps you are too young," Apollo said with a discouraged tone. "I don't think you are ready for it. I will report this news back to Guardian." Apollo turned to go.

"Wait!" Charlie yelled. I am ready for it! "Where is it?"

"Your breastplate is stored in a vault at a different location," Apollo answered. "A secret location."

"A vault like the vault of prayers?" Charlie asked.

Apollo's eyes widened momentarily as he started to say something then stopped. After a brief moment, he continued, choosing his words carefully. "Yes, very similar to that vault. We can discuss the similarities later."

Charlie took a hard look at the angel then said, "Well, let's go. I need to get my breastplate before it gets any later."

"Very well," Apollo said. "Follow me."

15

PLANS FOR THE HEART

"Is EVERYTHING READY for the boy?" Shirez asked.

"Yes, my lord," an assistant demon answered. "Apollo sent word he is near the place that has been prepared for the boy."

"Excellent," Shirez replied. "I expect constant updates!"

Charlie followed Apollo along a ridge that bordered the original trail he and Guardian had travelled. "You get a very different view from up here," Charlie said. "You can see the other trail and even the field that we changed. Isn't it amazing what faith can do?"

Apollo stopped. "That was you?" he questioned with a hard, angry voice.

"Yes," Charlie said. "Didn't you like what God did with it? Guardian said I'll meet the Sower again. Have you ever met her?"

Apollo bit his tongue, suppressing the words that were ready to boil out. "Yes, I've met the Sower," he finally said. "She has caused her share of problems around here."

"Problems?" Charlie asked. "What sort of problems?"

Apollo stopped and pointed to the landscape below. "Do you see all the territory below us?"

"Yes."

"Well, there are plans in place for each and every field. Every trail has a destination, every field an assigned crop. The Sower has no regard for the plans that have been assigned to the land you see before you. The Sower is a fool defying our instructions!"

Charlie pondered what Apollo said, "You mean, she does not consult God before she acts? Is that what you mean?"

"Yes, that is exactly what I mean." Apollo quickly added, "She is nothing but trouble!"

Charlie thought about the conversations he was having with Apollo. They almost seemed scripted. Apollo's answers were so short. His voice was not warm and deep like Guardian's, but scratchy and high-pitched. Charlie finally answered. "Well, you and Guardian seem to have very different opinions about the Sower, but I suppose that differences in opinions can happen even among angels."

Apollo quickly changed the subject. "Enough talk. We need to get your breastplate."

The two walked along the ridgeline until they came to the edge of a ravine. Thorns grew up both sides of the trail, forcing them into a narrow clearing at the edge. "What do we do now?" Charlie asked expectantly. "Are you going to make a bridge appear?"

"What a good idea," Apollo answered.

Charlie heard a thunderous crash, then a tremor struck the area. The ground beneath his feet shook and great cracks opened up. Charlie scrambled to avoid the gaping holes in the ground, but his feet fell into one. Pulling hard, he lifted his left foot out and tried to get his right foot out. Laying down his sword and shield so he could concentrate on his feet, he pulled frantically, trying to release himself. A violent wind attacked Charlie from behind, sending his shield and sword flying just out of his reach. The crevasse beneath his feet grew larger, swallowing up both feet. The earth seemed to be pulling him downward, all the way up to his waist. "Help me, God!" Charlie cried out. "Help me!"

Apollo grabbed his ears in pain. He recovered quickly as he reached out and seized Charlie, lifting his small frame out of the ever-increasing cavity. Then Apollo turned his face directly into the wind and commanded, "Be silent!" Just as suddenly as the storm started, it stopped.

Charlie scrambled after his sword and shield and yelled to Apollo, "What was that?"

Apollo answered with a sly smile, "Simply a storm. But as you can see, you do not need to worry when you are with me. You cried out for help, and I helped you."

Checking his armor to make sure he had everything, Charlie said, "Thank you! You certainly have violent and unpredictable weather here!"

"Yes, the conditions can be a bit surprising at times."

"Are we close?" Charlie asked impatiently. "I'd like to get my breastplate and get home."

"Do you even understand what the breastplate covers?"

"Well," Charlie thought for a moment. "It covers the front of your body."

"It covers your heart."

"Well, that makes sense." Charlie nodded. "You need to keep your heart safe!"

"Yes, that is where the plans are kept."

"What do mean *the plans*?" Charlie asked.

"All forward movement in life begins in the heart, where the plans are formed," Apollo answered.

"Do you know the plans for my heart?"

"Of course," Apollo answered, as he pointed to the bridge that had now supernaturally formed across the ravine. "The plans for your heart are stored in that vault just over there. Would you like to see them?" Would you like to see your future?"

"Would I ever!" Charlie exclaimed. "Let's go! I knew you would make a bridge!"

Apollo led the way over the newly formed bridge, carefully checking to make sure Charlie was close behind. When they arrived at the other side, Apollo pointed to a door imbedded within a rock face and said, "We have arrived, and now you will see the plans laid out for your heart!"

Charlie walked up to the door and looked for a place to use his Key of Truth but found that the door was already open. "Will I get to see what I will be like when I am older? Like what kind of car I will drive? Where I will live and things like that?"

"Yes, everything you want to know," Apollo answered.

Charlie slowly pushed open the door and saw a chair sitting in the middle of a dark room He walked over to it looking around for anyone else, but he did not see anyone else. Without warning, a red glow appeared on the wall opposite the chair. Charlie cautiously walked over and sat in the chair, keeping his shield and sword close and ready for action. "Okay, God, I'm ready to see the plans you have for me. I want to know what my life will look like as the Promise is fulfilled. I'm ready!"

The red glow came alive with a series of images. At first, Charlie saw himself, then he saw his family. Then the images changed, and he saw himself again; but this time, he was older. That image disappeared as a new one formed of him driving a brand new, upscale truck. That image paled, but another one took its place, showing his family together—all four of them. The last image that appeared made Charlie cry, because he saw his family laughing and singing in front of a Christmas tree. They were all together again.

Apollo walked over and stood next to Charlie, placing a heavy wing upon the boy's small shoulder. "I see you like the plans we have for you. If you agree with these plans, they can be for your heart."

"All I have to do is agree with them?" Charlie asked, as he wiped the tears from his face.

"We can give you this and so much more," Apollo said. "You simply need to agree."

"What am I agreeing to?" Charlie asked. "Guardian said that I have been chosen to reach the lost and to teach others. I did not see myself doing that. Why didn't I see that happening?"

Apollo ignored him, "Like I said, if you agree, you will have this and much more! Don't you want all that I have showed you?" Apollo almost screeched.

"I don't know. I really don't understand what I am agreeing to. Can you explain it a little better for me?"

"What I mean is that if you agree to our plans for your heart, then you will have everything your heart desires. Family! Money! Cars! Houses and more! You will be satisfied with everything you could possibly want from this world!"

"I do want all that stuff," Charlie said cautiously. "But is that part of the Promise?"

"Sort of," Apollo said impatiently, as he held up one wing and pulled an exquisite piece of armor from under it. "Behold your breastplate!"

Charlie gasped at the handsome breastplate, beautifully carved out of the darkest of metals. Charlie walked over and ran his fingers over the ornate inscriptions on the front. The words *Wealth*, *Power,* and *Prestige* were inscribed right where the breastplate would cover his heart. Charlie took a step back, feeling uneasy like something was wrong. Then he asked, "Where are the four stones that are on every other piece of armor?"

"Those will be added later," Apollo said.

Charlie felt uncomfortable and decided to pray silently, asking God to help him. As he did, he noticed Apollo becoming agitated and holding his head as if it was aching. At that point Charlie whispered, "Jesus, I need to see with my heart-eyes. Please help me!" Closing his physical eyes, he asked for God to help him see the truth. Suddenly, Charlie saw Apollo for who he really was—a repulsive demon. Charlie raised his sword and commanded, "In the name of Jesus, be gone!"

Apollo flew back against the cave wall then opened his mouth and started shooting flames straight toward Charlie. The boy held up his shield to protect himself, as he continued to pray for help.

Apollo screamed, covering his ears, and several other demons now surrounded Charlie, screaming at him to stop. Then they grabbed the breastplate, trying to force it over the boy's small frame. High-pitched chants surrounded Charlie. "You will wear this! You are ours! These are the plans for your heart!"

Charlie prayed as he took his stance. "In the name of Jesus, I will not wear your plans! I will serve God and no other!"

As soon as the words left Charlie's mouth, the ground shook and the door of the vault swung wide open. Charlie leapt for the opening, scrambling across the bridge as quickly as he could. The ground gave way, the bridge crashing down behind him faster than he was crossing. Mustering all of his strength, Charlie dove for the other side and tumbled to a stop among the thorns at the ridge. "Jesus!" he prayed, trying to catch his breath while he continued to run.

Turning, he saw countless angelic warriors descend upon the vault of the enemy and begin to battle the demons. "Thank you, God. Thank you!" Charlie cried out as praise lit the night. Charlie reached for his key in anticipation of needing it to cross back over. "It's gone!" Continuing his scramble to the top of the trail, he began to doubt his escape. When Charlie finally reached the top, he found a tree and slid down the trunk, allowing himself to rest and catch his breath.

The familiar voice of Guardian broke the silence. "Congratulations, Charlie. You passed the test!"

"The test?" Charlie asked. "I thought I was going to be captured and taken over by their evil plans for my heart!"

"But you were not captured, Charlie!" Guardian stated. "You've learned the power of the truth. Our God is stronger than the enemy, every moment and every day! You used the name of Jesus! There is power in that name, and there is power in prayer. You learned the secret of how to fight the enemy. What the enemy meant for evil, God has used for your good!"

Charlie thought about all Guardian said, letting it sink in. He recognized that he had become more comfortable with using his sword and shield. He had even realized when he needed to ask for help and see with his heart-eyes. "I guess I am learning how to fight the enemy, aren't I?"

Guardian's laughing approval warmed Charlie's heart. "Tell me, what made you realize you were dealing with the enemy? What made you ask to see with your heart-eyes?" Guardian asked.

"That's easy," Charlie said. "Their breastplate was dark and had selfish words inscribed on it. But the main thing was, it did not have the reminders of the sacrifice of Jesus upon it. You know, the four stones?"

"Yes!" Guardian said, grinning ear to ear. "Smart boy! I mean, superior warrior," Guardian corrected himself, as he pulled out a breastplate of righteousness from under his wing. "This one does."

Charlie had to shield his eyes from the brilliance of this piece of armor as he put it on. "Thank you." Charlie admired the craftsmanship and fit. Running his fingers over the four imbedded stones, he asked, "Can you tell me the significance of these marks right here where my heart is?"

"Yes, Charlie," Guardian said with a large grin. "Those are the fingerprints of God. You are His most excellent workmanship."

16

THE JOURNEY BEGINS

ECNAGORRA SECRETLY ENTERED the court, spying on the dozing Shirez, who had gorged himself with the power from the king's throne. "Over here," he whispered to the King of Lies.

"It is time!" the king commanded.

Swiftly, a squadron of demons descended upon the throne, completely obliterating Shirez into nothing more than a pile of ashes and smoke.

"Well done!" Ecnagorra complimented the king, as he bowed before him. "Now we must turn our attention to the Promise!"

"Guardian, can I go home now?" Charlie asked as he stood up. "I want to go home and see my mom."

"Yes, it's time," Guardian agreed.

"Oh, but, Guardian, I lost the key of truth!" Charlie was nearing tears. "I think I lost it when I had to jump for safety. You know, when the bridge was crashing down behind me. I'm sorry. I didn't mean to lose it!"

"Thank you for telling me," Guardian said, as he pondered the situation. "I will send a squadron of angels to scour the area and make sure it is not discovered by the enemy. As for you, your mom is waiting for you."

The entire court of evil was in disorder when a scout demon ran into the court, screaming about the destruction at the vault and that the boy had refused the plans for his heart. Furious, the King stood and screamed at his court, "Do something!"

Another scout demon entered. Immediately approaching the throne, he bowed down and asked for permission to speak. The king turned to his court to silence the chaos and gave the demon permission.

"My king, I have news! We have found the key to the Vault of Prayers!"

As soon as Guardian had spoken the words, Charlie was caught up in a violent wind and then set down in the same place—or it seemed to be the same place. Charlie walked a few feet and found the road that crossed through his property. Then he saw his house in the distance. He was home. Looking down at himself, he noticed all his armor was now just a memory. Charlie was not sure how long he had been gone, maybe just a few hours, maybe days. Charlie entered the house quietly, so he would not wake his mom and Sarah. He prayed that God would help him explain everything in the morning—he was going to need a lot of help. First Charlie stopped by Sarah's room to check on her and saw her small frame curled up in bed. Then he walked down the hall past his mom's room and saw the light still on. He knocked softly and whispered, "Mom, I'm home."

His mom, Becky, met him at the door, throwing her arms around her son as she sobbed. "My Charlie, my boy! You are home! I was so worried when I found out you had run away!"

"I'm sorry," Charlie said as he hugged his mom. "I was wrong, I'm sorry. Can you forgive me?"

"Of course," his mom cried. "I love you! I forgive you! I'm so glad you're home!"

"I want to explain, Mom," Charlie said, as he was silently praying for help to tell her the amazing story. "I want to let you know how wrong I was about you and Dad. I had no right to be so angry with you both."

"Charlie," his mom said, "let's just enjoy this moment of you being home. We have tomorrow to talk about all of that.

I have been on my knees praying for you since the moment I found out you left. Sarah was so worried she came to me after dinner to tell me what you had done. I called the police, but they said there was nothing they could do until more time had passed. I called all your friends looking for you." She threw her arms around Charlie and began to sob.

All of a sudden, they both heard the back door close. "That was the door, Mom. Is someone else here?"

"Just Sarah," his mom answered.

"I just checked on her when I came in. I'm going to go check on her again." Charlie rushed down the hall to her room. Charlie's mom followed, and they both reached across Sarah's bed. Something did not feel right, so they both pulled back the covers to discover she had stuffed her bed with pillows. Then they heard sounds coming from outside. They both rushed to see out the window and saw a small girl running toward the trail.

"Sarah!" they both cried out at the same time.

"Mom, I've got to go after her! She can't be out there alone!" Charlie turned to leave.

"Wait," his mom said, as she reached into her robe pocket. "You're going to need this."

Charlie held out his hand, as his mom handed him a key. "The key of truth?" Charlie said, hardly able to speak.

"Yes, my son." His mom had a warm smile.

Charlie stared at his mom for a moment, thinking how she had the key and what she might know, then he closed his physical eyes and looked at her with his heart-eyes and now he recognized her as the Sower. "Mom, it's you! You are the Sower!"

Smiling, she said, "Did you think you were the only one who knows Guardian? Now go! I will be on my knees in prayer for you both until you return!"

Charlie turned running down the stairs as fast as he could. He sprinted across the driveway and discovered Sarah had already crossed over to the trail, with the darkness swallowing up any evidence of her. Charlie wondered how she had been able to cross over without a key and then shoved his hand in his pocket, feeling for his key that his mom had given to him. Dropping to his knees, he prayed. As he was standing up, he held up the key, allowing the moonlight to light up the beautiful jewels, as a door suddenly appeared.

Charlie called out, "Sarah, I'm on my way!"

And so, the journey begins…

STUDY GUIDE

Chapter One

The King of Lies said that, "The Promise is upon us…"
*Review Joel 2:28–29 (*NASB*).*

1. What does it mean when God says he will pour out his Spirit?

2. How would this change your life if you felt God's Spirit poured out on you?

Chapter Two

"He wears my cape, and he is mine!"

1. Ecnagorra is the first demon we meet in this story. Do you know what his name stands for? Try writing it backward.

2. Why does the enemy conceal his true name in this world?

3. Do you believe that evil can root itself in your life? Are there scriptures that back this up?

4. Check out Matthew 13:37. It talks about good seed and weeds. What are you planting in your life?

Chapter Three

"Thank you! Thank you! Thank you!" Charlie said as he watched the power of praise light up the night.

1. Does praise really have power?

2. Support your answer with scriptures.

Chapter Four

"Stop!" Deception screamed. "You may have the boy. I have accomplished my assignment. Now the harvest!"

1. What are the characteristics of deceit? What would a *harvest* of deception look like?

2. How does the enemy use deceit in our lives to conceal his motives?

Chapter Five

"This is the great lie of the enemy. First, he will instill fear to keep us from moving forward, then he will make freedom look like bondage and bondage look like freedom."

1. Can you think of things that look like freedom but actually represent bondage? Think of becoming addicted to drugs. At first, it seems you can do anything you want. Then you become a slave to drugs. What other things look like freedom but are really bondage?

2. Can you think of things that may appear like bondage but are actually freeing? Think of money. The Bible gives us very specific rules about money. But we live in a society that says we always have to have more. Budgeting is a way to control your money usage and have money for the different areas of your life. Saving, spending, donating, and investing are the four pillars of proper money allocations. By following the rules about money in the Bible, you will develop a financial freedom. But the word budget sounds like bondage, doesn't it?

Chapter Six

"The Light works through those who are like children. The Light even states that a child can be the greatest in the kingdom of heaven."

1. What scriptures back this statement up?

2. What are some of the characteristics of children that are so appealing to God?

Chapter Seven

"Think of a shadow. A shadow is created by the light that shines around it. A shadow would not exist, except that it is the area the light does not hit. A shadow is darkness. Now you might carry a flashlight to help you see in darkness, so you know that darkness can be lit up by light. Can you carry a flashdark?"

1. What does the Bible have to say about light and darkness? Support your answers with scriptures.

2. Can you darken the light?

Chapter Eight

"The Belt of Truth is central to your character as a Christian. It is your posture."

1. What is your posture in the truth?

2. Can you recognize the lies of the enemy?

3. What is the best way to be equipped to recognize the lies of the enemy? Support your answer with scripture.

Chapter Nine

Charlie stood firm. Holding his sword directly at the demon, he said, "In the name of Jesus, I defeat you! Your lies and your evil must leave this place!"

1. This is warfare. This is using the power in the name of Jesus.

2. Does the Bible support fighting against the enemy by calling on the name of Jesus? Support your answer with scripture.

Chapter Ten

"Your feet have been shod in the Gospel of Peace…Your point of contact with the world is your feet. You need to approach life making sure the Word of God is at the center of your contact with the world."

1. What does it really mean to walk in the Word? Support your answer with scripture.

Chapter Eleven

"This is the gift of faith," Jesus said. "Your faith can break up the fallow ground and make a way for seeds of truth to be planted. The seeds can then grow and blossom. Then the air will be filled with hope, the aroma of Christ."

1. In this chapter, we see faith as both offensive and defensive. Is this true?

2. Give an example of offensive faith.

3. Give an example of defensive faith.

Chapter Twelve

"But when you see the Word of God in action, when you watch faith change the landscape from ugly to beautiful and meet Jesus in person, then the whole story of the gospel makes sense!"

1. Has this story made the gospel more real to you?

Chapter Thirteen

"Her name is the Sower. She reflects well the heart of Christ, and the Maker trusts her with seeds to plant and grow faith."

1. Do you know anyone who *reflects well the heart of Christ?*
2. Do they grow hope in the lives of others?

Chapter Fourteen

"Jesus liked to splash people," Guardian said.

1. How can you splash people with the Holy Spirit?
2. Give an example that you can use this week.

Chapter Fifteen

"All forward movement in life begins in the heart where the plans are formed," Apollo answered.

1. What does this statement mean to you? Do you think about things before they become actions and attitudes in your life?

Chapter Sixteen

"I'm sorry," Charlie said, as he hugged his mom. "I was wrong, I'm sorry. Can you forgive me?"

1. What difference does it make to say you are sorry to someone when you have done something wrong?

2. How does it feel when you receive an apology?

3. How does it feel when you need to apologize?

4. Is it important to forgive others when you are asking for forgiveness? Support your answer with scripture.

www.ingramcontent.com/pod-product-compliance
Lightning Source LLC
Chambersburg PA
CBHW071529100726
47908CB00004B/1332